Visions of Plum Street

An often true and inappropriate comedy
about Christmas and Skyline Chili

Billy Lambrinides

For my dad.

Thank you to my family and friends for making me laugh, and providing me with enough material to pass the laughter on to others. Thank you to my sister Debbie for taking the time to proof my words. Special thanks to Albert for his proofing, editing, and constant love and support.

ISBN-13: 978-1467978279
ISBN-10: 1467978272

CHAPTER 1: A TURKEY

I think every holiday story should begin with a nervous breakdown, so let's start there. Christmas comes earlier and earlier every year, particularly for me. For the last 10 years I have been in magazine publishing, with most holiday issues being produced a few months before they actually show up on the newsstands in December. I am usually decking some halls for a photo shoot in August, or prematurely cooking up some holiday recipe to taste and review for the readers. Well, this year was going to be different, because I quit my job at the magazine to become a serious writer. I'm not even sure what that means, because I'm not a terribly serious person, but something inside me said I needed to do this.

I had to do something. When I am walking to work and jealous of the homeless lady begging on the corner, the gardener blowing leaves, and anyone else that doesn't have to sit in a slave-cubicle all day long, it's time for a change. I could push a shopping cart into the center median of traffic and make art with crayons in the sunshine all day, wearing all of my clothes at once, and talk to myself too. Hell, I'm typing to myself like a lunatic right now, so I'm halfway there. Plus, I'm sure there are just dozens of millions of careers I haven't even attempted yet. I was unchallenged at work and my boredom had surpassed the maximum limit. I was miserable, so I decided to quit before I became the crazy guy going postal with a gun in the office. I mean, that idea suddenly made total sense to me, just to end the monotony for everyone. I wasn't just leaving my job on a selfish whim; I was leaving my job to save lives.

Now, how was I to know the career change should be to become a writer? This I'm still not so sure about, but I knew I had something inside me that I needed to get out. I was filling up with ideas and, strangely, as a result, I started getting fat. The body is an amazing thing when you listen to it. I was mentally filling up and not doing anything about it, so my body showed me the obvious. That and I started to have weird dreams about poop. Yes, poop.

One night I dreamt that I was sitting on the toilet and making number two. Before wiping I looked between my legs and found that I had pooped the letter 'O'. I told my friend Johnny this and he asked, "How do you know it's the letter 'O' and not just the natural swirl of the bowel in the bowl?"

"Johnny, it was my dream. I know when I'm pooping a letter and when I'm not. Why in the hell would I just dream of a normal poop? I'm not some freak having fecal fantasies all night." Let me just add that I am not judging, if you, dear reader, by no choice of your own, happen to normally dream of poo.

"Plus, the next night I dreamed I pooped the letter 'N'. It was a capital 'N' with pointy angles that I would have never naturally done. This was followed by a 'C' on the third night, and an 'E' on the fourth. I put them together and realized that I pooped the word 'ONCE'.

Johnny looked at me with disgust, and just enough intrigue that I continued.

"'ONCE Upon a Time' Johnny! One way or another, my body was beginning to tell a story, a crappy fairy tale, literally, but a story nonetheless. I think I'm supposed to be a writer."

"...or a high-colonic technician," Johnny deadpanned. "Also, note that if your body continues to crap the story, it better start using lower case letters, or that thing is going to be a bitch to read, and to get out for that matter."

"Nope, the dreams stopped as soon as I figured out the message. The rest is up to me I guess. Johnny, I'm going to be a writer, possibly a crappy one."

I realize that as a man pushing forty this is equivalent to me saying I want to be a prima ballerina or a cowboy, but with utter confidence and complete stupidity, I gave notice to my boss. Then the economy tanked. I now feel completely responsible for the collapse of the world financial system. I've heard that we are all necessary cogs in the machine, but I didn't realize that me leaving my art directing post at a small, car-enthusiast magazine would have such a huge domino effect. I'm having serious guilt issues, but I have to finish what I set out to do before I can figure out a way to pull America out of this recession. This world monetary mess shouldn't affect me as a writer because as long as I have paper and a pencil I can go to work, but it certainly makes not having a regular paycheck a bit more daunting.

I do some blogging to warm up and try to figure out what I'm supposed to tell you about and I procrastinate. In Los Angeles we call this procrastination "research and development". I do some yoga, write some short stories and dilly dally a bit when I get a call from my friend Mark asking me to help with a benefit show he's involved in.

"Billy, I'm going to be Miss Alabama in the *Best in Drag Show*," Mark says with his southern accent. Mark's twang has actually gotten heavier over the last 15 years we've known each other.

"Mark, you're from Tennessee, not Alabama." I respond.

"I'm playing a character, Holli Daye, a southern belle completely obsessed with Christmas, who lost her voice in a freak hunting accident."

"Wow, that's specific. You've really worked out the background details of Holli, you method actor, you."

"It's not that subtle. I plan on doing the beginning of the show using one of those tracheotomy voice box machines. Then I'm going to regain my voice through a Christmas miracle during the show and burst into song. I could really use your help with some of the props and sets for my act."

5

"It sounds tacky, tasteless, and over the top. I'm in. Please tell me though, how does hunting tie in with Christmas?"

"Well, Holli is trying to save a reindeer when she gets shot in the throat with an arrow. So, I also plan on doing the beginning of the show with the arrow still intact. Like the old Steve Martin bit, but lower, so instead of the arrow poking my brain, making me 'wild and crazy', it pierces my larynx, and makes me mute. "

"Of course."

With no nine to five to go to, no story immediately screaming in my head to tell, and charity calling, I agree to help out. I first research the Aid for AIDS' *Best in Drag Show* to find that the annual over-the-top benefit is bigger than I imagined. It's a one-night-only, all volunteer, extravaganza, which in the past has included huge sets and live camels on stage. Whatever I make, and let me remind you that I am not a carpenter, it has to be good. So, it is the beginning of November and I am building a Santa sleigh and a huge nativity scene, again diving into Christmas long before anyone else is; this time, diving into a feather boa, sequined, cross-dressing Christmas.

As I'm sawing away at large pieces of plywood in my garage for Mark's sleigh, I decide that maybe it's best to make my first story something with a holiday theme. I mean, I've practically just become one of Santa's helpers, so it's probably best to stay in Christmas mode to keep from going schizophrenic. So, I think about story ideas as I hammer but, quite frankly, California doesn't seem like the ideal location for a winter tale. I think it confuses people. Sure, we have snow, but it's fake and they shoot it off the roofs of mini malls to subconsciously cool the shoppers down. It's some sort of sudsy chemical snow that kids actually catch on their tongues like the real thing. First you see their little faces light up when it starts to faux snow, out come the tongues, and then they start spitting. Instead of an icy treat, they get their mouths washed out with soap by God. People even attempt to look like a typical catalogue-Christmas here, shopping in hats and scarves over their tank tops and shorts. I have to admit it's a bit odd for the uninitiated, but there is nothing more fun than going to an outdoor shopping center like The Grove and watching the Victorian carolers sweating out songs under layers of heavy wool. Everything is decorated with lights and garlands, but we still have roses blooming in the yards and the temperatures are ideal. This is not *the* typical winter wonderland, but it is certainly *my* winter wonderland, and there is plenty of magic to be found here.

I remember my first holiday in Los Angeles when I was living with my friends Trisha and Michael, both of whom had made the move from Cincinnati to the left coast with me earlier that spring. We decided to kick off the season by hosting a huge Thanksgiving for the new friends we had made, but we were completely unprepared. We were young and independent, and none of us had cooked a bird before, let alone an entire pilgrim feast. We also did what most singles do the Wednesday night before Thanksgiving: we went out and got tanked. I was actually driven home by the nice and incredibly attractive bartender who had been pouring me drinks all night, only to get out of his jeep and puke all over the sidewalk. Trisha and Michael had a similar night out on the town, and Trisha ended up inviting a guy she was interested in to join us for the dinner. We all woke up Thanksgiving morning, green with hangovers, headaches all around, with a huge meal to prepare. I remember specifically that I was working on the cornbread stuffing next to Trisha, who was going to prepare the bird. Trisha was smoking a cigarette with one hand and cleaning out the cavity of the turkey with the other. I was stirring a big vat of wet bread, which looked exactly like what I had left on the sidewalk the night before, and I started to dry heave. Trisha then began to poke at the poultry with a hard stick of butter that she had just pulled out of the refrigerator.

"Trisha, I think you have to soften the butter first, so you can coat the whole thing. Try to work some under the skin too."

Without a beat, and with a smoldering Marlboro hanging out of her lip, Trisha picked up her cigarette lighter and flicked it at the end of the butter stick. She then rubbed a bit on the bird and continued the process of lighting the butter and rubbing it on the bird, lighting and rubbing. I was still trying not to get sick, and I suppose I could have suggested that Trisha use the microwave directly behind her, but her method seemed to be working. We were not the Norman Rockwell picture of Thanksgiving. We decided that the hair of the dog was going to be the method of choice to get us through the day, and started drinking as soon as the bird was in the oven. We drank and cooked, laughing all day long, and I could tell Trisha was loaded before the guests arrived. I knew this when she insisted on mashing the potatoes with an electric mixer and ended up coating herself and our kitchen walls with the lumpy spuds. Her inebriation was further proved when, halfway through the meal, Trisha slid under the dinner table and promptly passed out. This is when the date she invited over the night before arrived.

"Hi, I'm Kevin. I'm sorry I'm late, is Trisha here?"

"Well, yes and no." I responded. "She is physically here, but I'm not sure if she's mentally available."

Kevin began looking around the table and then got a puzzled look on his face.

"Lower. Look lower," I said laughing, "She's resting under the table."

So, Kevin, being the sport that he is, climbed under the table to greet his date. We finished the meal and I remember putting the mutilated turkey carcass into a kitchen cabinet to get it away from Trisha's cat. The garbage was full and I was drunk, so this seemed like a good idea at the time. The party continued until late in the night and, big surprise, I again woke up with a splitting headache. I walked through our filthy, potato-wall-papered apartment, climbing over passed-out bodies, and headed to the kitchen in search of rehydration. I went to reach for a water glass and when I opened the cabinet I was surprised to see the turkey body that I had left there the night before. As I began to pull the platter off of the shelf, I thought it seemed rather heavy for a plate of dry bones, but nothing registers properly when your brain is swollen. Then I saw something move in the turkey, something furry. With that, Trisha's cat jumped out of the turkey cavity and onto my face. I didn't know what it was; I just knew that something alive jumped out of something dead and scared the living shit out of me. Let me be clear, that would be the living shit and not actual shit, although I may have farted a little.

Now, I know what you're thinking, "How in the hell is this drunken story magical?" Well, would it help if I told you that Trisha and Kevin have been happily married for about 15 years now and have a lovely baby girl? No? I suppose it doesn't have enough yuletide splendor yet, so I'll continue to blabber to you as I try to figure out how to make this sleigh hold the weight of a large southern drag queen. Also, moving forward, I will try to speak less of poo and vomit.

CHAPTER 2: TROUBLE

The next morning, I continue sweating in my garage as I screw casters under Mark's giant sleigh blades, so the thing will glide across the stage properly. My phone rings and I see it's a call from my sister Debbie. Immediately I get a strange feeling in my stomach like something's wrong. I guess you have to understand how communication happens in my family, particularly because of the three-hour time distance between California and Ohio. My mom is the matriarch of the family, immediate and extended, and all communication goes through her. We talk weekly to mom about what's going on in our lives and she tells us what the other one's are up to. I get a full report on all activities concerning my three sisters, three brother-in-laws, seven nieces and nephews, and all of the aunts and cousins my mom hears about. I'm not a big phone person, so this system has worked for years. When it's a random call from my sister, I get suspicious.

"Hey Deb. How's it going?" I ask casually.

"Oh fine," she replies, also trying to sound like nothing is out of the ordinary, "but I'm going to put Sherry on speaker phone with me."

I froze. One sister on the phone is bad, but two sisters on the phone at the same time is trouble. That's trouble with a capital T, which rhymes with P, which stands for Parents. Something bad has happened.

"What's going on?" I ask, "Is it Aunt Katie?" I learned from the last conversation with my mom that my aunt was having some heart trouble. This was a stretch for me because I already guessed that a problem with my aunt would have only been a one sister call.

"It's dad. He's in the hospital. Mom said she woke up last night when dad fell on his way to the bathroom. He's lost a lot of blood and he's in serious condition."

I didn't know what to say and I didn't want to cry over the phone. I could tell they were trying to hold it together themselves, and I didn't want to be the baby to break the floodgates open. "What happened?" I asked. I thought I could get the two words out but I heard my own words breaking as I said them.

"Dad fell in the bedroom and called her name, and she found him on the floor covered in blood. She tried to drag him to the bathroom because he was bleeding so badly, but he was too weak to move and too heavy for her to lift. She called 911 and the ambulance arrived in minutes to bring him to the hospital. They're up there now, trying to stabilize him."

"Jesus. Ok. What should I do?" I said, trying to hold back another round of tears. "I guess I should get the next flight home."

"No, don't do anything yet because mom didn't even want us to tell you. Just pray." Sherry said.

"What do you mean? Why didn't mom want me to know what happened?"

"Because, she knows that if you found out, you would immediately fly home." Debbie finished her thought, "...and if you show up at the hospital, dad would think he's going to die. Just stay put until you hear from mom."

I'm apparently like the grim reaper. I show up and people assume they're on their way to the long dirt nap. I'm like Oscar the death cat from that nursing home some years ago. That left one question unasked. What happens if, God forbid, dad does die and I'm not there? I hang up the phone and sob. I sob for dad in the hospital and I sob for mom, knowing she is there watching her husband hold on to life. And I pray. I pray to every saint, and every dead relative I can think of. It's my nature to hope for the best but to prepare for the worst, so I try to only hope. I am broken and I am half way across the country from the parts that needs fixing.

This is not the first scare we've had with my dad. Just a year ago at this same time he started throwing up blood, a lot of blood. He did nothing about it because each time he got sick, he felt better afterwards. This is how my parents operate – they self-diagnose and as long as they're feeling fine at that moment, everything must be all right. So, my dad was coughing up blood for two days and passed out before they finally called an ambulance. He kept saying it was just something he ate. I told him that was unlikely unless he had been snacking on shards of glass. He blamed a sour pickle. Yeah, a sour pickle rolled in shards of glass maybe. They stabilized him at the hospital, but they couldn't ever find out what the problem was. I remember they even had him swallow a camera-pill, which is technology I didn't even know existed. The miniature digital device sent over 500 images to a large belt he wore for a day. Because the camera thankfully was not reusable, it could just pass on out of him. I was told that he just had to check and make sure it came out, so it didn't cause damage to his system. A few days after he had the procedure and we were waiting for the results I was talking to mom on the phone about what had happened and asking if dad had passed the camera or not. I heard her screaming across the room to my dad,

"Bill! Bill! Did that camera ever come out of you?"

"How in the hell am I supposed to know?" he screamed back to her from his lounge chair across the room.

"You have to check every time you go to the bathroom. Have you been looking after you go?"

"Hell no. I'm not doing that."

"Well, I'm certainly not doing it." she said, this time to me.

"Mom, if dad doesn't check he's going to have to go back to the hospital for x-rays."

A few days later my dad was back at the hospital getting x-rays. The camera had exited his body, for a polite way of putting it, but the results of the procedure showed nothing. The problem just went away, only to return now, a year later.

I am now realizing that I promised last chapter I would speak less of vomit and poo, and I did try, but to clarify, I did not promise to speak less of vomiting *blood* or pooping a *camera*. I am now also realizing if I ever want this story to become a Christmas classic, I am going to have to lighten it up. I'm not sure if they ever talk about bodily functions in *The Polar Express* or *Rudolph*. It will surely never be animated for kids. I can't picture projectile spewing of blood being done in stop-motion clay, although it would be very dramatic on sparkly white snow. Tim Burton could pull it off maybe, but I'm getting ahead of myself.

While I worry and wait to hear more about dad, I'm just going to tell you some more about my memorable Christmases. Also, in case you're interested, I am painting Mark's sled bright red with glittery candy cane runners. It's looking pretty good and it's the only thing helping me take my mind off of bigger problems.

The same weekend that we roasted the bird and toasted our

brain cells, Trisha, Michael, and I decided to decorate for our first Christmas in LA. We had always had artificial trees growing up in Ohio but decided that there was enough make-believe in this town, so we would splurge for a real Douglas fir. The three of us were sharing a dingy apartment and our budget was tight, but it was something we all wanted that year. We went to the Mr. Greentrees lot across from the Hollywood Bowl and picked out a tall beauty for our living room. We strung the lights and hung the bulbs, each of us contributing ornaments from our childhoods, and had a dazzling Christmas tree glowing in the front window. I remember that tree. I remember it, but not for any special or unusual way we decorated it.

That Christmas I got wrapped up and stressed out with shopping. It was the longest I had been away from home, and I wanted to bring really nice gifts back for everyone. I had myself worked up into a tizzy about it. I remember shopping, all in a panic, with my friend Mark and overhearing a lady talking to her daughter and saying, "This will make a nice little gift for the mailman." The mailman? I'm supposed to get a gift for my mailman? I don't even know if my mail carrier is a man or a woman, let alone what to get them. I also remember getting home from that long day of shopping in a very bad mood and walking up to our apartment door, a warm glow coming from the window. Hanging on the doorknob was a gorgeous silver and white angel ornament. Attached was a note saying this: "Here's a little something to add to your beautiful Christmas tree. I'm your neighbor across the driveway and I don't get out much anymore. Your tree has really made my holiday special. Thank you."

I cried, because that's what I do apparently. Some stranger made my day and woke me up to what was important. I don't remember one present I got that year or one that I gave, but I will never forget that tree with the beautiful angel.

Mom finally calls me later, and she sounds drained. She tells me what my sisters already told me but adds, "It looked like a murder scene. You're father lost so much blood but he seems do be doing better. They put a scope in him. They found the problem."

Oh those four beautiful words. I could suddenly breathe again. "That's great news mom! What's going on, and when should I come home?"

"Well, he had a bleeding ulcer and two lacerations, all of which they cauterized while they were doing the scoping. I don't know how they did it, but it seems to be working. Your father still has a way to go though, he's very weak." She goes on to tell me the details and I can tell she's exhausted with worry. She's still trying to comfort me, but I know she needs as much comforting as I do.

"Mom, I can be on the next plane home if it will help."

"No, your father is going to be just fine and you're coming home next month for Christmas anyway. I know you're working on projects for Mark's show and probably have Thanksgiving things to do."

"Mom, none of that matters if you need my help. Plus, I'm just going to be here worrying about dad anyway, so maybe I should just come home."

"Sweetie, you might as well worry there because at least you'll be helping with your friend's charity stuff. You can't do anything but sit in the hospital room here, and your father has plenty of company. I could probably use your help more at home later when dad's out of the hospital anyway. Why don't you just come home early for the holiday instead?"

We go back and forth and decide that I'll return to Ohio at the beginning of December. The *Best in Drag Show* is

Thanksgiving weekend, so I'll get to follow through with the commitments I made and spend turkey day with friends before flying out. So, it's back to the garage and on to gluing red gems to a sleigh.

CHAPTER 3: THE SAN FRANCISCO TREAT

I'm still in the garage, and now working on a large foam-core nativity scene. Mark asked me to make a manger big enough to hide behind but light enough to carry, as an entrance for one of his numbers. His face will be sticking over the top of the manger, crowned with a headpiece that makes his face look like the star of Bethlehem. I don't know how I get myself into these situations where I find myself painting donkeys and glittering wise men. For shits and giggles I decide to make Jesus a pop-up figure, so Mark can flip a lever in the back and have the baby rise out of his crib. It's not often that you get to turn the birth of a savior into a comedy bit.

Of course, part of my head is still in Ohio, but the other part is fine-tuning the giant creche. It starts to drizzle outside, very unusual for this time of year in Hollywood, but it reminds me of another California Christmas, this one in San Francisco. Trisha is now married to Kevin, and the three of us all move into a flat together on Pierce Street in the Lower Haight. The flat below is occupied by a nice quiet couple and their boy. The building was newly renovated, and the family had chosen the bottom flat to avoid the stairs, a poor choice if you require quiet, because you will hear people walking above you in an old Victorian. The boy seemed shy to me, and a little lonely. This was at the height of the dot-com boom and there were not many children in the neighborhood because young families had been priced out. Noise had become an issue with our neighbors and I could feel a weird energy growing between the floors. We were generally not loud people and made every effort to keep the volume down.

I remember at one point the neighbor coming to talk to us about noise and suggesting, "Why don't we all make an agreement to not wear shoes in the house?" I think my response was, "I'm sorry, but we don't care if you wear shoes in your apartment because we can't hear you anyway, and we're going to continue to wear shoes in our ours. We have rugs down and we're not wearing taps on our shoes, and quite frankly, I don't like asking guests to remove their footwear. I think that's odd. I don't really like taking my shoes on and off either." Then we just stood there looking at each other awkwardly. I was just going to blame Trisha, because she's the one that wears the heels, but I didn't want to throw her under the bus because of her footwear. I also reminded them that they chose the bottom flat before we even moved in. I remember the boy looking mortified by his dad's request. My guess was that he felt alone enough already and could see that his parents were pushing us away.

Otherwise, we are loving our gorgeous new apartment and excited to see the Victorian dripping with garlands. I don't think there's any style of home that looks better when decorated for the holidays, probably because of *It's a Wonderful Life* and *Meet Me in St Louis,* which both feature Queen Anne's. It's been raining for weeks in San Francisco, and Trisha, Kevin, and I are getting anxious to go buy a tree but don't want to get soaked doing it. I actually get my holiday shopping done early, and find that I have an extra present. It's nothing really, a little metal BluesBand harmonica in a vintage box. I was considering adding it to a present for my nephew, but I ended up buying something else for him altogether. I rack my brain thinking of what to do with it, and think of the neighbor below. While the parents have been rubbing me the wrong way, the kid seems nice enough, so I decide to wrap it up as a surprise. Not wanting another encounter with the parents, I decide to do it all anonymously. I sign a card from Santa, and slide the tiny package in their mail slot when I know they're not home.

I remember getting a surprise gift when I was a kid. I received a phone call telling me to check the front door and there, tucked inside our screen door, was a beautifully wrapped box with no card, no tag, no clues of a sender. I tore it open to discover a toy train engine, which made noises, lit up, and rolled around the ground without tracks. The gift was cool, but the mystery was intoxicating. I am still not exactly sure who gave it to me. Using the process of elimination and vague voice recognition from the unexpected phone call, I am now 90 percent sure it was from my Uncle Christy, my dad's twin brother. That still leaves 10 percent uncertainty, 10 percent magic. It continues to rain in San Francisco.

After another week of non-stop drizzle, we decide we can wait no longer to buy our Christmas tree and head to the tree lot closest to our house. It's called Delancey Street Trees, and I recognize the name as the group that helps reintroduce ex-cons into the workforce. They have a successful restaurant in the city, which does great work, but I hadn't planned on dealing with hard-core drug addict rehab-ers for my tree buying experience. It's pouring rain, and we are being helped by a gigantic black man who easily may have killed someone. We slowly walk through the selection of wet trees, most bound tightly with string, easy places to hide dead bodies. When we decide on the tree we want, the possible murderer screams to another ex-con, "Trim this one up, Benny!" Out of a dark corner comes another gigantic man, this one Latino, wielding a chain saw over his head. He's moving quickly towards us and starts up the weapon with a pull on the cord, making a loud metal grinding noise, drowning out both the rain and the holiday music. Trisha, Kevin and I instinctively scream. Real blood curdling shrieks. The screaming eventually turns to laughter when we realize that he's going for the tree trunk and not our heads, and he starts laughing also. All of the men working there ended up being big teddy bears, but there is nothing scarier than an ex-con coming at you with a chain saw in the rain.

We drag home our wet Douglas fir, carry it up to our flat and begin to decorate. I remember that I've left some bulbs down in the garage so I head downstairs to look for them. As I'm digging through boxes, our neighbor comes down to start some laundry, also in the garage, and I'm waiting for him to make some comment about how loud we were.

"I've been trying to figure out who did it." he says.

"Who did what?" I respond, assuming we'd been too loud, whatever it was we were doing.

"I've been trying to figure who left my son a harmonica in the mail, the only mail with no postage, the only mail we've gotten recently from Santa."

"I'm sorry, but I don't know what you're talking about." I smile. The first rule of Santa Club is that you don't talk about Santa Club. Anonymous means just that.

"Well, I think you do. It's been bugging me this whole last week, and we just don't know that many people in this city. I've eliminated everybody I can think of, so I'm assuming it's one of you."

"What kind of harmonica?" I ask, still smiling, trying to throw him off my scent.

"The kind you blow in. Look, I know you did it, and I'll keep your secret."

"You claim to have gotten something from Santa and I'm not Santa." I said.

"I'm trying to thank you and you're making it very difficult." I wasn't trying to make it difficult for him to apologize. I was trying to make it easier for him to keep a secret from his son.

"You don't have anything to thank me for."

"Well, thank you anyway," he says, "You brought a fun mystery to our house, and really made my boy happy. I think he's been feeling a little isolated here, and now he knows he's not alone. At least Santa is watching. Also, I want to apologize for our noise complaints recently. I realize that I'm sounding like a crotchety old man, and neither of us wants that. Plus, my wife has been enjoying your Christmas music."

"Well then, you'll have to join us for some more music and a drink as we finish decorating our tree."

I remember the confused look I got from Trisha and Kevin as I walked into our flat with the nasty neighbors from downstairs. I was smiling from ear to ear, and I whispered to Trisha, "Santa took them off the naughty list. I'll explain later."

CHAPTER 4: A DRAG

I'm not sure what to call myself when people ask. It used to be 'designer,' followed by 'singer/actor,' and most recently 'art director.' I am now saying 'writer' because that's what I'm doing, even though I'm not getting paid for it. It sounds better than 'eater' or 'sleigh-maker,' my other activities of late, which I'm also not getting paid for. Normally it doesn't matter what people think of me, but I'm having lunch with my partner Albert and an ex-boyfriend of his, who I naturally want to impress. The three of us are chatting and the ex, David says, "Billy, I heard you quit your job. What are you doing?"

"I'm writing," I spit out in a panic, already knowing his next question.

"Oh. What are you writing, a screenplay?" Everyone assumes you're writing a screenplay if you live in Hollywood.

"No, I'm working on a Christmas story." With this, David scrunches up his face like he just smelled a big fart. Oh my God, just the thought of a Christmas story made him noticeably grimace, like I made him eat poo. Sorry gentile readers, maybe you would prefer I say "grimace, like I made him eat a sour lemon" but the face was more like I made him eat poo. I didn't know what to do, so I continued, "It's going to be a memoir or a collection of short stories, I'm not sure yet."

"I don't really read. I only know DJs and music," David finally said. This is my audience, so I really don't know why I bother.

David continued, "It's all about Christmas, really?" Again, his face scrunches when he says the word. "So it's a book, you're writing a whole book?" I don't think he's ever read a whole book, so I have blown his mind. This is not a difficult feat.

"I'm not sure, maybe I'll just write half a book, sell it for cheaper and leave the end open for interpretation." I do not say this, because that would make me an ass.

"Well, it's going to be mostly comedy," I say, realizing that I'm now talking like I might to a child. I consider telling him that it might have pictures, even though I know it probably won't. "David, nobody reads," I say politely, "but if it's any good it will become a television show, a movie, and eventually, hopefully a Broadway musical."

"I hate Broadway musicals."

I give up.

I go home and return to my writing, which will never be read, about subject matter that people don't really like. I now realize that by writing about Christmas, I am seriously limiting my readership. Maybe I can throw some Jews or atheists into the story. Please note that Jesus was a Jew and if I happen to mention my very good friend Gabi, he's a Jew. I decide to put the finishing touches on Mark's sleigh and manger instead of writing any more that day.

After much preparation, the day has come for the Aid for AIDS *Best in Drag Show* that Mark is competing in. Let me just interrupt myself for the grammar nuts out there to say that I know you're not supposed to end a sentence, like the last, with a preposition like 'in,' but that's how the voices in my head speak. I arrive early, as I am part of Mark's pep squad, to pass out jingle bells and urge the audience to cheer for Holli Daye during the show. Of course, Mark initially told me, months ago, that he wanted me to be a sexy Santa. Since that time, I have somehow been demoted to elf, and now finally a Christmas caroler. So, it's my first time at this huge event downtown at the Orpheum Theater, and I arrive looking like some sort of holiday party reject. I'm wearing red and white plaid pants, a festive vest, and an iridescent fur-trimmed Santa hat, which is making me sweat profusely. Why do I do this? There are hundreds of very attractive people walking by in appropriate clothing, enjoying alcoholic beverages, and not acting like a carnival barker. I am belting out Christmas carols in November, looking like a sweaty person with no fashion sense. Thankfully the room is also filled with over twenty men dressed in dog drag. Yes, dog drag. They are some cross between 60's modern glam-woman and afghan dog, which is frightening to both species. Apparently a big opening number with a chorus of dog-women, led by a drag queen who does a free standing back flip, has become the tradition of the show. Don't ask.

I should also note that I am mingling, singing Christmas

tunes with vulgar lyrics, and sweating among the likes of Molly Shannon, Jennifer Coolidge and John C Reilly. At one point I'm in the lobby ringing bells, and singing something nasty to the tune of "Up on a Rooftop." My dear friend Trudy Savage, who has been a children's agent in town for about a hundred years, comes up to say hello while I'm mid-carol. She is standing a foot away from my face, trying to hear over the crowd, expressionless. I can't tell if she's shocked by the lyrics, or if it's just numbness from years of plastic surgery and painkillers. I realize she's having trouble hearing, so I sing louder, "Ho Ho Ho, She is a Ho. Ho Ho Ho, She is a Ho-o."

Trudy still can't hear, so I'm yelling, "Up on a rooftop, click click click, Down through the chimney...."

And the music cut's out as I scream "...she tucks her dick!" spitting the words into Trudy's stone cold face.

"Jesus. I get it already," she tossed at me as she turned to take her seat.

The show begins, and it is a total blast. I am sitting behind Kathy Griffin and Charlie Sheen, both regulars at the event, and I can see why. The seven contestants include a very fat

Miss District of Columbia, Cherry Blossom, who makes one of the most dramatic entrances of the evening. He is flown in like a ghetto Wonder Woman driving an "invisible," clear, inflatable lowrider to the stage. There is also a Cuban Coco Lopez from Florida, and Miss Kentucky's Phiddle-de Dee. The best joke of the evening comes at his expense and goes something like this. "He's just like KFC. Once you've eaten the leg and the thigh, all you're left with is a greasy box to put your bone in." They are also competing with a set of conjoined twins named Karen and Sharon Livers as Miss Tennessee, but only Karen wants to be there. Sharon is hysterical dead weight.

Mark makes his entrance for the swimsuit competition in a working snow globe. It is one of those huge lawn decorations which has been refitted so that Mark is actually walking surrounded by the thing, lit from within, snow blowing around him, and dragging an extension cord from off stage. It's hysterical and the crowd goes nuts. His next entrance is in the giant Santa sleigh I built, which wheels out on casters and is trimmed with neon tubing. His final evening dress for the competition is a true metamorphosis spectacular. He begins the descent down the stage stairs behind the huge nativity scene I designed, with his face serving as the star of

Bethlehem. He gets to the bottom, and with a flip of a lever, the baby Jesus pops out of his cartoon crib. Mark steps out from behind the nativity with the top of the star still on his head, serving as a tiara to compliment his gigantic gold ball gown. Just when you thought you'd seen it all, Mark jumps into a headstand, and the entire dress flips upside down, turning into a life-size Christmas tree! The same star from the beginning is then jammed on his high heels to top the tree. That, my friends, is how it's done.

I am proud to say that our contestant Mark comes in a very close third place for the night. He is only beat out by a cheerleading Tara Ligament and a white trash Shelby Free. Shelby got her name because she was so ugly at birth her momma said, "She won't even be able to make $20 on the streets. Shelby Free." Tara takes second place with her competition song "Oh, Mickey" which began as a slow piano concerto and escalated into a high-energy cheer. Shelby takes the top prize with his macramé and beer-can evening gown and his outhouse-inspired swimsuit. Over $350,000 is raised over the course of the evening because everyone volunteered to pitch in and help for free. It's like one of those Judy Garland and Mickey Rooney movie musicals, where they put on a show to save the day. You make the costumes, I'll build the props, someone else sings a song, and soon enough you have a show. And what a show it is. It's rare that something as funny, vulgar and politically incorrect as this can have so much heart.

I get home from the event and call my mom on the phone to tell her about the evening and find out how dad is doing.

"Your father seems to be doing well, but he's very weak from all the blood loss. He's responsive, but he's lost a lot of his mobility, so we need to move him someplace for therapy. I can't bring him home like this. Your sister is going to talk to her friend Dan who runs a place to see if they can get him in for a while."

I'm pretty sure that my mom is talking about a nursing home, but she never uses those words. She can't.

"Well mom, I think that's a good idea. I don't want you hurting yourself trying to take care of dad. I'll be home next week, and hopefully dad will be back home by then too. I can handle any of the heavy lifting from that point on." I then steer the conversation back to the drag show to try to get her voice from a quiver to a laugh.

CHAPTER 5: SWEET CHARITY

"I need your help at the nursing home, Billy. I usually have church people come to the activity room on Sundays, but they're going to be out of town for the holiday. Do you think you could help entertain the group and lead the singing of some Christmas carols?" The normal voice of my friend Raul on my machine, a heavily accented combination of Mexican and toothy-gay, sounded desperate.

I usually like to keep my Sunday mornings free, for hangover recovery or church. By church, I'm referring to coffee at home listening to Rufus Wainwright, followed by brunch with friends drinking screwdrivers. There is nothing that will bring you closer to the Lord than that, but I knew I would probably have to forgo church for charity this weekend. With my dad going into a similar facility in Cincinnati for rehabilitation, there was no question that I had to do this. It's strange when you suddenly feel like you're on the right path, particularly when it's not a path you intended to be on, and in this case, one you don't necessarily *want* to be on. Had I not quit my job, I would not have the opportunity to go back to Cincinnati for so long to help out. Now, I find out that my father is going into a nursing home, and a friend calls the next day and asks me to help him at a nursing home. What are the odds of that?

"No problem, Raul. My high school show choir used to entertain at convalescent homes, and I used to sing on cruise ships, so I'm actually quite experienced with the elderly." Some of my best audiences have been crapping their pants while they're clapping their hands. I suddenly feel as if I have a noble purpose, like I am going to entertain the troops, well, the troops from World War II maybe, but the troops nonetheless. I am going to use my small sliver of God-given talent to give back to the community and kick off the Christmas season, even if it means a morning of caroling through old people smell.

I ask my manfriend Albert if he will be joining me for my big charity extravaganza, but the idea is hitting too close to home for him. Albert's 94 year-old grandma Fanny was recently put into a similar facility in Nevada, and he has been dreading his holiday visit to Carson City for that reason. One of the first weeks Fanny was put in the home, she asked where her husband Joe was staying while he was visiting. She had seen him the night before. They had to explain to her that Joe, Albert's grandfather, had died 20 years earlier. Dead Joe apparently also told Fanny that her sisters would be coming to see her as well. They, of course, are also deceased, and the idea of this thrills me to no end. I am fascinated by any sort of "crossing over" story, and this one was happening to someone I actually know and love. I will spend an entire hour crying to John Edwards on television, and am addicted to everything psychic or paranormal. But this was different. This episode was starring Fanny, not a TV audience member, clearly being prepped for a heavenly take-off.

I arrive to Fountain View Rehab and Nursing Center in Hollywood and find Raul serving coffee in the activity room. I do not see a fountain, which I'm sure confuses people. Raul is buzzing around fifteen wheelchairs, trying to energize the decaying bodies in them with his friendly spirit. I am trying to not breathe and wondering if I would be able to sing and not inhale.

"Mmm, smells like Christmas!" I joke. "Hey, I thought you

weren't supposed to serve them coffee because it makes them pee too much," I ask as he continues his hosting duties.

"True, the nurses don't like it, but my seniors get whatever they want when I'm working. Shit, I'm considering sneaking in some weed and booze for some of them, so coffee is the least of my worries." Raul is a saint and a java rebel. Again, I fear I may have to remove the dope reference if this is to become a holiday classic, but for now I want to tell the story as it happened. I don't want to lie to you, nice readers, even if it makes Raul sound like a drug addict, which *is* debatable. Also remember that this part of the story is taking place in California, and marijuana is merely medicine, like really funny chicken soup.

I make small talk with two pretty young Latin girls as we wait for our piano player, Neva, to join us. Raul is now barking back and forth from English to Spanish trying to keep the seniors awake. "Now, we're going to write Christmas cards to our families who visit us." Most of the patients can barely keep their heads up, and few want to pen greeting cards for the free people not in the senior slammer.

"Don't you want to write a card for your sister who visits?" he asks an attractive older black woman. Her hair is nicely done up and she wears bright red nail polish. I realize she must have been a real looker in her day. Even now I don't know if she's 70 or 100, because black people simply don't show age. The saying is true: black don't crack. This immediately makes my white ass feel like I'm wrinkling as fast as a time-lapse photograph. We exchange glances as she pushes the card back to Raul, rolling her eyes, and we both start laughing. Clearly this sister does not like her sister, and will not be messing up her polish for correspondence. The rest of the group sit around a long table waiting for my big show, or to die, toss a coin.

Neva arrives, and I immediately like her. She looks far too young to be here, but I notice some open sores on her hands, so maybe she's here for recovery. She talks like a battleaxe rehearsal pianist. "Let's start this show before we go into union overtime," she chuckles, and tries to plug in an ancient keyboard. I stand next to her in the front of the room, and we start singing through the Christmas songbook. I'm singing and watching the seniors watch me. Their skin is paper thin and wrinkled, but if you just look at their eyes you can see their souls. You can see what they may have been before arriving here. Some of them are singing along, and some are just peacefully listening. There is a Mexican lady who sings every song, and her smile already has made my day. Neva is getting excited about the music and tosses me a set of jingle bells to play along. Throwing a gay some bells is like tossing us a tambourine. Neva and I go quickly, one song into the next without a break, like we were doing an ABBA medley. The seniors go crazy. By crazy, I mean several woke up and one stopped drooling.

We wrap up the show and Raul walks me out, thanking me for my help. "What do those two Latin girls do that were in the room watching me sing? Do they do what you do?" I ask.

"No. They do something else, but stayed to hear you sing. Do you want to know what they said about you?"

"Sure." I said, assuming it would be some sweet compliment about my performance.

"The shorter one said that she wants you to fuck her for three days, and the taller one said she wants you to fuck her standing up."

"Jesus Christ! I was singing 'Oh Holy Night.' That is not quite the response I was expecting. Well, I promised that I would sing, but that's as far as my charity is going...and if I do ANYTHING for three days, I'm not doing it standing up."

Now I am wondering what the old people were thinking when I sang 'It Came Upon a Midnight Clear.' Raul had told me in the past that the elderly masturbate all day long because they're bored, and now this. I was practically raped while I was singing Christmas carols, and I didn't even know it. Even stranger is that I got one of the hottest compliments of my life at a nursing home, at Christmas, from *girls*. I wonder if any of the original drafts of *The Christmas Box* talked about doing the nasty. This is why me being a serious writer seems very questionable. Oh, and I'm now definitely ruling out the idea of doing children's books.

CHAPTER 6: SILENT FLIGHT

Albert and I both leave for our respective Christmases, mine in Ohio and Albert's in Nevada. I'm boarding the plane behind a group of deaf kids, probably in their early 20's. They're a really cool looking group, three Asian guys and two pretty girls, one of them Chinese, and one black, all dressed far hipper than I am. They look very metro-international, like they could model for a fragrance ad. I can't stop watching their hands, which move like a beautifully choreographed dance. I hope they don't think I'm eavesdropping, even though I don't know a word of sign language. I am fascinated by deaf people, but I must admit that it freaks me out when they actually speak aloud, like Frankenstein's monster. I'm watching them and listening to them talking to each other, and they start to laugh at something. It's the first time I realize that the noise of laughter is completely universal. There isn't a deaf laugh, nothing freaky or out of the ordinary, just joyous noise, like everyone else's laugh. Well, everyone but my friend William who brays like a donkey, and my friend Carol, who's laugh is so high it can break glass.

As it turns out, I end up sitting next to the group, myself in the window seat. I normally introduce myself to whomever I sit next to, so they don't think I'm a terrorist. I'm Greek, have a shaved head and a goatee, and I know my look intimidates some people, particularly on airplanes. I scribble down on a piece of paper, "Hello, my name is Billy" and show it to the black girl with a doo-rag on her head. She politely looks at me with a half smile, like I am a complete nerd, a creepy older nerd, to be specific.

Well, I have a side story to tell, which is really tasteless, but true. I wasn't going to tell it to you, because it's that tacky, but the deaf girl has driven me to it with her ageism, or her possible terrorist-nerd-hate. I hesitate to tell it, because it involves an Academy Award winner who I am quite fond of, and who happens to be really sweet. I waited tables on her once, but that's another tale, and a side story to my side story is too much. See, that's the thinking of a serious writer.

That first Christmas in LA, years ago, which I've already chatted at you about, I knew a guy who worked at the Pottery Barn at the Century City mall. He was seasonal help, and one afternoon in the middle of a busy holiday shopping frenzy, he was approached by Marlee Matlin. He looked at her, completely unaware of who she was, and asked, "Can I help you find something?"

"Eim ook een or ee urkey adder." Marlee asked. Yes, I am trying to type phonetically deaf, and yes, I know I'm going to hell.

"Um, I'm sorry, what is that you're looking for again?" he responded.

"Eim ook een or ee urkey adder." Marlee asked again.

"Yeah, I'm sorry, I'm still not sure what you want," he responded. By this time a small group had gathered closer, as people tend to do with celebrities. Their star power has an actual gravitational pull.

"Ei unt u urkey adder." Marlee asked again, still ridiculously patient.

"Nope, I have no idea how to help you..." the guy said, trying to brush off the lady.

He was interrupted by the store manager, who had been observing the conversation and was now in full panic mode. She yelled across the store as she approached them, "Turkey platter! Turkey platter! For the love of God, she wants a turkey platter."

I do believe that was his last day at the Pottery Barn, and rightfully so. I warned you about that one, and my apologies to any of my deaf readers, and to Miss Matlin. I do hope you will play yourself in the film version when this story becomes a holiday spectacular.

I'm flying home and thinking how nice it is to sit by deaf people instead of a crying baby or a Chatty Cathy. I then start to worry about my dad and wonder if he's going to be home when I arrive, or if he's going to still be at the rehabilitation place. I cry myself to sleep and slumber for much of the remainder of my journey. I'm awoken when the deaf people get into a heated fight, their hand movements shaking my seat like it's on vibrate. It's not the good 'magic fingers' kind of vibration, more like an earthquake tremor. Their silent, passionate debate is shaking me so violently it would kill a baby. I'm now taking back what I said earlier about sitting by the deaf. There are no good seats on an airplane.

My brother-in-law picks me up from the airport, and he gets me up to speed on the situation at home. I had hoped dad would be out of the nursing home, but it sounds as though he needs more rehabilitation. I'm also warned that mom has her bridge club over, so the house will be filled with ladies. I get dropped off into the den of aunts and mother hens that I've known since I was a baby. Everybody acts as if everything is completely normal, even though it's not. The energy in the house feels totally different to me. Dad is missing. Worse than that, dad is somewhere that he shouldn't be, like prison. I want to get in the car and drive to where he is, but it's late, and I have no idea where he is or how I would spring him out. Mom gives me a hug and kiss, and pulls me aside.

"Your father is still at Dan's place," she says.

"Dan's Place sounds like a bar. Dad knows he's in a nursing home doesn't he?"

"Well, he's still a bit out of it, but I think he knows. It does sound like a bar, which your father would prefer, and they do have a free Happy Hour. They also have free popcorn, which your father won't stop eating. Really, anybody could come in off the streets and have free drinks, apples or ice cream, and nobody would know the wiser." I inherited my rambling from my mother.

"Mom, I don't think people are sneaking into a convalescent home for the free stuff. They could give away lobster dinners every night, and I still don't think people are going to want to while away the hours at your fake senior bar. Can I go and see him now?"

"No, it's too late, your dad's asleep. We'll go first thing in the morning. I should warn you though: your dad is awful company. He doesn't say a word, and doesn't want to be there."

"Mom, I wouldn't want to be there either. In fact, I don't want to go there. We're supposed to give him company, not the other way around."

"You'll see what I mean. He's awful. The nurses all love him, because your father is always the most polite man. They prod and poke him with needles, and he just says 'thank you.' They all want to hug him and kiss him and he just rolls his eyes."

True, my dad doesn't say a ton, but he's a great listener, and that's what people need. Plus, my mom and sisters are always talking, so he rarely has the opportunity to speak. None of us do. I'm lucky that people really do love my parents, not just my sisters and I, who *have* to love them, but strangers love them too. My parents are completely likeable. My mom will talk anybody's ear off, and she often does, and my dad is always a calming energy to be around. I'm not surprised the nurses adore my dad, and I'm sure my mom knows as much about each nurse as she could dig out of them.

CHAPTER 7: FRANK AND SENSE

The next morning we have some breakfast and head to Dan's Place, also known as Hillenbrand Rehabilitation Center. It's weird, but I have passed this building a million times and never knew what it was. We only see what we need to see, and I never needed to visit this place. I'm glad it's not called a nursing home, even though that's what it is. It's not home. Rehabilitation sounds hopeful at least, and this one has a salon in the lobby, so some people just come to nurse their hair back to health I guess. "I'm going to Dan's Place for Hairbilitation" a swanky ad might read, or maybe, "I recovered from a triple bypass *and* had my roots dyed, all while enjoying free popcorn at Hillenbrand!"

We walk past the lady at the front desk and say our 'hellos' and mom grabs a green apple from the basket. We have a full basket of uneaten apples in our kitchen, all pilfered from Dan's, but mom can't resist free things. She's a Depression era baby, so is much better prepared for this global financial downturn then I am. I suppose I should start stealing senior fruit. We then walk into the large elevator and mom plugs in a security code to make it move. It is like jail. You have to use codes, or the old people will just wheel themselves out in the streets. I actually saw that, years ago when I lived in Los Angeles. There used to be a nursing home across the street from Johnny Rockets on the hippest part of Melrose Ave. I was enjoying a burger when I saw an old man try to escape. The whole restaurant cheered him on as he wheeled himself into the slow moving traffic and tried to cross the street. He was huffing and puffing so hard, you would have thought he was crossing a state line, not just an intersection. Like, if he could just cross that mental border, he could enjoy the rest of his days basking in the freedom of the malt shop. After struggling for twenty minutes, he got about 9 feet, before some attendant came and pushed him back. It was all very exciting.

We get to the room and I see a man in a wheelchair sitting outside. He gives me big smile like he knows me, and I smile back to be nice. The man starts to say something, but turns his chair and shakes his head before wheeling down the hall. My mom gives me another warning before we go in: "Your father repeats himself a lot. It will drive you nuts, so be patient." Both of my parents have repeated the same stories to me for years, so I'm not sure how to respond. I take a deep breath and slowly enter the room. Dad is sitting on the edge of his bed, dressed and ready for the day, in track pants and gym shoes. He looks weak and noticeably older, but he gives me a big smile, so I know we're going to be okay.

"Billy! How are you? This is bullshit." he says.

"Dad! I'm doing great. You're right, it is bullshit, but it beats the alternative. I'm glad you're feeling better."

"Bill, did you get a shower and put on clean clothes?" mom asks dad. Mom buzzes around the room making sure everything is where it should be.

"Yes, I did. I'm not sure what time it was because it was dark."

"Great." she says. I'm not sure if this is great in a sarcastic way because he was up too early, or actually great that he's clean. "You got a shower and put on clean clothes?"

"Yes." he responds to her and then we continue to chat between ourselves. Not five minutes goes by when my mom looks at my dad and asks, "Bill, did you get a shower and put on clean clothes today?"

"Yes!" we both yell. Jesus Christ. I'm not sure who is going to drive whom nuts first with all the repeating. One of us is bound to snap, but they have patience and practice on their sides. I help dad into the bathroom and mom looks at me while we wait, "I know he didn't put on clean clothes because he was wearing those yesterday. I was repeating the question so he would fess up."

"Mom, dad's a little out of it, and can't totally distinguish day from night right now. I don't think he's trying to pull a fast one on you. He believes he got a shower and put on clean clothes, which is fine."

She screams into the bathroom, "Bill, did you get a shower today?"

With that, I have to take a break. They are completely insane, which is normal, so I have to assume recovery is going well. I walk down the hall and into what appears to be a recreation room. Everyone is either in a wheel chair or has a walker parked next to them. I sit down at an empty table and close my eyes to think. I'm approaching 40 years old, which means I'm about the age that my father was when they had me. He's 81. At my age, my dad was married with three teenage daughters, owned a home, and was part of a successful restaurant business. I have a cat. I still can't figure out what I want to be when I grow up. Oh, and there is no more growing up, just growing out, which makes me sad and fat. As I type this I also realize I'm the biggest narcissus ever. Sorry, 'narcissist', not 'narcissus', which would make me a flower. I can't even think about my dad without it turning into me me me. To be fair though, all of the wonderful things that I think and know about my dad, I'm keeping to myself, because that's how we operate. I make fun of him, and that's how he knows I love him. I don't want to get all nice and have him think that I don't care. So, I'm meditating on being a sad, fat, narcissist, when I get poked in the arm.

"It IS you," the old man says as he pokes me in the arm with his cane. Again. "It is you, so it is him. I thought so, but now I know."

"Hi. Do I know you?" I have no idea who this man is, but he is in a wheelchair and has a cane, which seems redundant.

"You look just like him. You look like both of them actually." Old people are weird. I have never seen this man, yet he thinks it's just fine to wake me from my sadness with the prod of a stick and harass me.

"I think you may be confusing me with someone else. Everybody thinks I look like someone they know with a shaved head and a goatee. "

"Nope." he says and just keeps staring at me. I suppose I have to be nice to this man, because if he dies soon I don't want to be the last dickhead to ignore him. He will certainly share that news when he gets to the other side.

"Mr. Lambrinides, I suppose?"

"Wow, Yes, but nobody calls me that. It's Billy. I'm sorry, but have we met?" Now I'm really glad I didn't ignore him, because he knows my name. He actually pronounced it correctly as well, so he didn't just read it somewhere. I often get Mr. Lamborghini but usually just Mr. Lamb, because there are just too many letters for people to figure out after that. This is a reminder to myself to use short words from here on out.

"No, we haven't met. I'm sorry I'm staring, but my vision

isn't 20/20 anymore. Has anybody told you that you look just like your dad, and your uncle for that matter?"

"Well, yes, back in high school when I still had hair, our pictures looked similar. Do you know my dad, would you like to say hi?"

"I knew the boys a long time ago. No, I don't want to bother him. That's Bill in the room; your father is Bill, right? I had read that Christy passed away a few years ago."

Christy was my dad's twin brother, yes, brother. I have never met a man named Christy, but that was his legal name. My yaya and papoo, my Greek grandparents, had five sons, and they would be 'the boys' this stranger is referring to. My grandparents apparently had some weird ideas for naming children. Worse than a boy named Christy is the oldest brother, my uncle. His name is actually Lambert Lambrinides. Who does that to their child?

"Yes, Uncle Christy's gone. That's my dad, Bill, in the room. How do you know him?"

"I wouldn't say I know him. I would say that I knew him. I knew them when we were all still boys, a very long time ago. I was their neighbor on Plum Street for a couple years. I doubt your father would even remember, it was a very short time in a very long life."

"I've certainly heard a lot about the apartment on Plum Street. In fact, I worked around the corner from there at an ad agency for a while."

"This was long before the advertising firms were in the neighborhood. This was when Cincinnati was commonly called Porkopolis because of all the livestock trade on the river, and it smelled like, well, pig shit. I knew the boys when downtown was still alive and bustling, and we were all poor."

"Dad still thinks he's poor. I'm bad with names, but if I remember any of the stories he's told, I bet you're part of the Italian family that lived above them."

"Why, yes, I am. Frank Salamone is the name. Your dad was quite the crack-up. He's a good person."

Frank seemed surprised to be remembered. I really can't recall anything specific dad said about him, other than he liked all the neighbors. I love old stories, particularly when I know the players, so I thought I'd share what I know and see what he can fill in.

"There were two of you, right? Dad said he used to be friends with a younger son that he would bum around with, and an older one who used to take them places."

"I'm the younger one. My older brother, Vito, passed away years ago in the war. He was in the Air Force and his plane was shot down. My parents never quite recovered from that. You may have heard stories about them. Mama, Maria, was good friends with your grandmother, and pop used to work with your grandfather. "

"I'm sorry about your brother."

"Boy, you have nothing to be sorry about. Thank you, but that was long before you were even around."

"Dad used to tell me that Yaya used to be friends with the neighbor woman. Yaya could only speak Greek and the neighbor could only speak Italian. He was always surprised how well they got on, hands constantly moving, like a never ending game of charades."

"Well, they also both had children that spoke English to be translators," Frank says, laughing.

"Did you say that your father worked with Papoo?" I ask.

"I didn't say that because I don't know what a papoo is."

"Sorry, Papoo was Nicholas Lambrinides, my grandfather."

"Yes, they worked together for a while at The Emperor. It was a greasy spoon with a royal name, owned by a real asshole. Behrens, was his name, Marty Behrens. I remember he was tall and skinny, just bones of a man, and a terrible cook. Dad used to say that he was so thin because even he didn't like to eat the food he made. Your papoo was an excellent cook, though."

"I never met him. He passed away before I was born. My parents are both fantastic in the kitchen, and I'm not so bad either, so, thankfully, I think it's in the blood. It's nice to meet someone who knew my dad when he was a kid, he doesn't talk about it much."

"Your father was never a kid, more like a funny old midget," Franks says laughing again, "There was no play time for kids like today; we worked."

"Yes, I know, uphill both ways," I responded dryly.

"Well, we did walk to and from school, if that's what you're referring to, but it was flat. We really worked. Your father sold newspapers on the corner of 3rd and Vine, and always had chores to do." Frank paused like he remembered something and continued, "To be fair, when I saw your father for the first time he was playing. When we pulled up to the red brick Plum Street apartment, I remember looking up to the fourth floor unit, which would be ours. On the third floor fire escape, I saw two boys that looked exactly like each other with big ropes tied around their waists. I had no idea what to make of it."

"I heard my yaya used to tie them to the fire escape because she was afraid they would fall off," I added. I'm not sure which would do more damage, just the three-story fall, or the three-story fall with a rope around your waist. A rope, which upon impact, would surely turn into a giant cheese-slicer. Ah the good old days, when you could still tie up children.

"Yes, that was quite a sight. They looked like a twin acrobat team ready to perform. Your dad waved and Christy was singing I'm sure. He was always singing" Frank said, his voice getting slower.

"Really? I didn't know that." This was the first completely new bit of information for me. "I was a professional singer myself for a while. I guess I got my voice from him."

"They were identical twins, with the same voice, you could have gotten it from either of them. Your uncle loved to sing and rarely shut up, but your father hated the attention."

This is true, he prefers to listen rather than talk, and then occasionally throw out a zinger. Not to bring my narcissistic self back into the situation, but I had always wondered about my singing voice, because it seemed to come from nowhere at all. I could tell Frank was getting tired, but I now had questions for the man.

"Frank, I have to get back to dad, but I wouldn't mind talking some more if you have time later."

"In here, we never know how much later time we'll have, but I'm not going anywhere."

Uncle Christy was a singer? Maybe this is just a crazy old man who isn't remembering clearly, or maybe he knows more about my family history than I do. Well, now I have questions for dad, and pieces of a puzzle to fit together. I can't believe I just wrote that, like I'm solving some Nancy Drew caper.

CHAPTER 8: GREEK TO ME

Dad spends the afternoon in and out of physical therapy and rest. It's nice just hanging out with him, but I can tell conversation isn't high on his priority list. He wants out of this place, but the doctors still think he needs a couple more days to recover.

I start asking questions about his days on Plum Street, and he confirms that Frank and Vito were the names of the neighbor boys that lived above them in the apartment. He tells me that Frank was a sickly kid, a couple years younger than he was, and Vito was a photographer. He also tells me that a woman named Lillian Fowler lived on the second floor below them. She had a daughter and a German shepherd but dad couldn't remember her having a husband, so maybe she was a widow. This was the late 30's, so I certainly hope she was widow and not, oh my God, divorced. How scandalous, to have a single woman with a bastard child living below and wild Italians living above. Plum Street got even more exciting when dad told me that Nick Batsalis, another Greek, ran a tailor business on the first floor. He used to make clothes for the kids and spent most of the day smoking hookah pipes.

"Hookah pipes?" I ask, surprised.

"Yeah, hookah pipes, and let me tell you, it wasn't just tobacco he was smoking. There was definitely cocaine, or opium in those pipes."

My parents, thankfully, know nothing of drugs, but I doubt the tailor was smoking cocaine or opium. While opium sounds exotic, he would have been too messed up to make clothes, and coke, which is rarely smoked, would make him too fidgety for delicate needlework. Weed. Nick Batsalis, my dad's childhood tailor probably smoked dope. Finally, a character I can relate to, because if I had to make clothes for a bunch of screaming poor kids, I would have to get high, too.

"Pot? You had your clothes made by a stoner?" I ask excitedly.

"If that's what he put in those pipes, I guess I did," dad says, laughing.

It's weird, while dad's short term memory is on the blink, his long-term memory seems to be better than ever before. I've heard lots of stories about Plum Street but even he's telling me new details. I decide to dig for more information about his early newsboy career. I, of course, am thinking about the 1992 musical *Newsies,* starring a young Christian Bale, and am hoping my dad's experience could compare. In my head, there needs to be a musical number here.

"Yahtz was the name of the paper guy we worked for on 3rd and Vine. There was a Jewish man that sold newspapers on 4th and Vine that was pissed because we stole so much business." See, look, all my non-Christian-friends-reading-a-Christmas-story, another Jewish person.

"How did you do that?" I asked.

"Well Christy and I made quite the team. Identical twins, dressed alike, and we put on quite the show."

"What? Quite the show?" I was kidding earlier about the musical number.

"Sure," he continued, "I would tell a few jokes, mostly dirty one's I'd heard around town, and your uncle would sing songs." Holy shit, I get a musical newsboy number, and confirm that Uncle Christy was indeed a singer.

"Uncle Christy sang? You never mentioned that."

"I guess it never came up, or I forgot."

"What else do you remember about that?" I pried some more.

"We would sell papers for five cents, and get to keep three cents for each one we sold. Yahtz liked us because we were the cleanest boys in town. Some of the other newspaper boys were filthy, but your yaya was particular about cleanliness. She would do all the wash herself and had a wringer in the back yard to help squeeze it dry before she put it on the line. Yahtz was kind of crazy though. One day he dumped a huge stack of papers on us because we had sold so much the day before. When we complained that we couldn't sell that many he said, 'Then eat them!'" my dad says laughing. I don't get it. Maybe that would be considered a funny joke in the 1930s to a young boy, but it's not working for me now. I decide to move on to other topics that may prove more entertaining. Most of the stories I already know, but let me catch you up on some of the more interesting, relevant ones before I move on.

My papoo and yaya, Nicholas and Alexandria were both born in a small Greek peasant town called Kastoria. Isn't that a pretty name, 'Alexandria'? She had no dowry, both were poor, and they were matched to be married. Actually matched, like "Matchmaker, matchmaker, make me a match." So again, if this story is ever to become a musical, insert a similar song here, like that one from *Fiddler on the Roof*. My friend Gabi and I always comment that there's not much difference between the Greeks and the Jews anyway. They decided to start a new life in the United States, and in 1912, a teenage Nicholas left alone for the new country to search for work and a place to settle down. I can't even imagine moving at that age to a new country, with no work or relatives to greet me, not speaking the language. Alexandria stayed at home in Greece with her family until Nicholas could send for her. He landed on Ellis Island with all the other huddled masses yearning to be free, but knew that New York City was not to be their final destination.

He quickly found work as a cook for a railroad crew, which would take him on a journey west, and build up his savings to bring his young wife abroad. Apparently being on the railroad crew was rough work, and there were many fatalities from dysentery and influenza. They would regularly come to the cook, who served as a sort of site manager, to find out how many in the crew died. My Dad always tells me with pride that whenever they would approach Papoo and ask how many he lost, his response was always, "none." Every other crew was losing men by the dozen because of lack of general hygiene, but Nicholas was keeping his men alive with techniques he brought with him from Greece. He would wash everything thoroughly, and bury waste under shovels of lye, which others weren't doing, so he was asked to teach his cooking and cleaning methods to the other crews. But cleanliness isn't what he claimed saved lives. It was the garlic. Nicholas cooked with lots and lots of garlic, and was always heralding the healing properties of the cloves.

With his success working on the railroads, he began sending money back to Greece so his wife could join him in America. For years he was sending his hard earned dollars, but little did he know, Alexandria's family was enjoying the cash cow, and keeping the money for themselves. Can you believe that? My great grandparents were apparently greedy shits. The railroad took Nicholas to Cincinnati where he found a small Greek community, so he decided to stay. At the time,

Cincinnati was a bustling town, bigger in size than Chicago because of the Ohio riverboat trade. He found work in a hotel kitchen and was ready to settle down and start a family. It had been 10 years since he left, and again he sent money back to Greece, this time with a warning that it would be his last attempt to bring his wife to the new country. My great grandparents realized they wouldn't be getting any more money mailed their way, so Alexandria was finally sent to join her husband in Cincinnati.

They moved into the Plum Street apartment, and did what most newlyweds did, even after ten years of marriage. They had babies; and these babies would become know around Cincinnati as 'the boys.' First was Lambert, the oldest, who's hair was always standing straight up in the air. He had constant bed head then and still does today. Then came Jim, the gambler, who could usually be found rolling the dice or playing cards on some street corner. Next came the twins: Christy, and my dad, Billy. Last, but not least, was Johnny, who would be the artistic one in the group. When he was a kid though, he was apparently obsessed with flying. Howard Hughes had recently broken the transcontinental speed record, and my Uncle John would spend an entire day sitting in a cardboard box behind the steering wheel of his imaginary H-1 flyer.

Not long after Johnny was born, the hotel closed down where Papoo worked, and he took a job cooking at The Emperor chili restaurant. I should tell you, in case you're not familiar, that chili in Cincinnati is it's own animal. It's different than Texas chili and different than anywhere else in the country. Cincinnati chili is a meaty sauce, spicy, but not hot, usually served over spaghetti. Emperor chili was not what you would call Cincinnati chili today, it was it's own concoction also, mostly bland. Well, now that I've given you a brief history of my family, I will move forward. I normally wouldn't tell you something so unfunny and extraneous to this Christmas story I'm attempting to write, but I do think it's rather interesting stuff: matchmakers, immigrants, and railroads, oh my.

CHAPTER 9: THERAPY

The next day I am again visiting dad at Dan's Place, still not a bar but wishing it were. Dad is also wishing it's a bar, because he wants a Chivas on the rocks and not the juice or soda they keep offering him. Neither of us wants to drink just the mixers without the booze. It seems like a silly waste of time, all this hydration.

I walk with dad down to the therapy room where he has his rehabilitation. It's basically a gym for the seniors, where they have stationary bikes and treadmills. The only difference is that most of the patients wear straps across their bodies, in case the trainers need to catch them during a fall. I don't know what would be worse, just falling on the floor, or being caught going down, yanked like a yo-yo by a full-body safety belt, back onto a machine. Dad takes his spot on the bike that's not going anywhere, and rolls his eyes.

"Dad, do you want me to stay while you have therapy, or come back in an hour?"

"Get the hell out of here while you still can," he says very dramatically, like the star of a horror movie. I already knew the answer before I asked it, because the only thing worse than working out in senior straps, is someone watching you. Thankfully dad still has his sense of humor.

I only have an hour to kill, which is hardly enough time to leave and come back. I begin digging through a stack of magazines in the reception area, and discover they are as old as most of the patients in this place. I read a two-year-old Redbook, but decide I can do something a bit more useful with my time, like try to spread a little sunshine in this place. I'm going to mingle. Raul told me that seniors masturbate all day long, so I'm a bit worried that I will run into old people doing the nasty everywhere, like the worst porno imaginable. If this is ever to become a musical, there needs to be a big senior sex production number here, like the song 'Contact' from Rent. Hot hot hot heat, sweat sweet, wet wet wet, red heat. Instead of young East Villagers writhing around, it's old West-Siders with walkers and wheelchairs, all backed by kick-lines of dancing Viagra and Cialis.

Still, there have to be some lonely people in here, without things shoved in their private parts, who would like to chat. I walk the halls and smile, trying to avoid looking in the rooms, checking out the rest of the facility. I get down one hall, and decide that my large smile must look totally fake, which it is, so I move to a lesser, half-smile. I don't want the seniors to think I'm an extremely perky person; nobody likes that, particularly here. Happy, perky people make the seniors do things they don't want to do, like have sing-a-longs, or bathe.

By the time I get to the third floor I have barely a smile at all, just a lift on one side, with no exposed teeth. I pass a room and notice Frank in his wheelchair, eating graham crackers that he pulls out of his shirt pocket.

"Hey Frank, do you have the Keebler elves working in that shirt pocket?" I ask loudly to get his attention.

"No, and you didn't see me eating anything, if anyone asks." This is all the more funny because he could not possibly have more crumbs on him if he tried.

"Frank, your secret is safe with me. Do you want some

company?"

"Well, I suppose I could put off watching *The Real Housewives of New Jersey* until another day if I must."

"I talked with dad yesterday, and he was reminiscing about Plum Street. He said that your brother Vito was a photographer, but I thought you had told me he was in the Air Force."

"Well, yes I did and yes he was. He was a photographer in the Air Force. When your dad knew him though, he was just learning photography, and was getting some freelance work with *The Cincinnati Enquirer*. What do *you* do, are you in the family business?"

"No, I'm not, and I'm still trying to figure out what it is that I want to do." I hate when people ask me what I do. It never defined me when I was working, and now it's just a great big elephant in the room. People want to mentally file you away by your career choice, and no one knows where to put me. *I* don't know where to put me.

"Are you on drugs?" Frank seriously asks me.

"No, I'm not on drugs, Frank. I am just having a slight mid-life crisis."

"Well, I guess you're around the age for it. Are you going to get a sports car?"

"No, I'm not into cars. I'm not even doing my mid-life crisis properly. I was going to get a tattoo, but the idea of paying someone to stick me with hundreds of needles filled with dye isn't up my alley either."

"What is up your alley? What do you like to do?"

"I love to cook, but I'm afraid if I made it a career choice that I would eventually hate it. My favorite things to do are eating and talking, but there is not a lot of work or growth potential there."

"True." Frank continues, "I thought you said you were a singer. Why not do that again?"

"I love performing, but I already did it, and it's not the life I want to lead. You have to give up all your nights and weekends because, unfortunately, that's when people want to be entertained. There is not a big demand for singers that want to work the nine to five shift; not to mention the fact that people want to have beautiful young 20-somethings singing to them, not moderately attractive 40 year olds."

"You're lazy and spoiled."

"Thanks Frank, you're old and mean, so I guess we're even. What's wrong with wanting more from your life than what you already have, or what you already know?

"Nothing I guess. It seems to me that the luxury of choice is keeping you from doing anything."

"Frank, were you a therapist when you were younger?"

"No, just a listener. Therapy is another luxury for your bored and spoiled generation. Let's cut to the chase. What do you want to accomplish, what can you do to make money?

To me those are two very different things. What I want to accomplish, usually doesn't make me much money.

"I want to write. I do write actually, and have had some articles published. That's what I'm working on, a story."

"Neat. What kind of a story?"

He is the first person that didn't look at me like a leper when I told him I wanted to write. "I'm working on a collection of

Christmas stories, mostly comedy, but I'm stalled."

Frank now looks at me with the squished face of someone smelling a fart that I have come to expect when mentioning my Christmas tale.

"Christmas just isn't that funny. Don't get me wrong, I'm a big fan of Christmas, but it doesn't seem like comedy material. Maybe you could start with a dramatic or sad holiday story, to warm you up?"

"Well, that's great advice, Frank, cause everyone is going to want to read a depressing Christmas book." I say dryly.

"I'm just thinking it might be more relatable." I like this Frank, and someday in the future hope to write a holiday tale filled with horrible loss and misery, just for him.

"I'm actually thinking about writing a story about the apartment on Plum Street. Some sort of historical fiction, because I've always liked that time period." The words come out of my mouth without thinking, something I don't like. If I had just thought about it and never said it out loud, I could write anything. Now I feel obligated by my voice to get this particular story down on paper.

"You're a romantic if you're looking back at the Depression as the good old days. They were the tough old days and certainly not filled with comedy."

"Frank, the toughest days of my life have also been the funniest, in hindsight. You and my dad seem to have survived it all and are still laughing."

"True enough. Well then, let's get to work." Frank says abruptly.

"What do you mean, let's get to work?" I ask. With old people, you never know, if everyone is on the same page.

"I have a story to tell you, one that already exists about Plum Street. You will also be happy to hear that it takes place around Christmas. I can't promise you that it's funny though."

I am stunned. How could there be a story about Plum Street, let alone of the Christmas variety, that I haven't heard. Frank could be completely full of shit, or riddled with dementia. Either way, the words have been said, 'I am going to write a story about Depression-era Cincinnati,' which I know nothing about. Then, just as soon as I put the idea out in the stratosphere, a weird old man offers to help. Again, I feel like

I am on the correct path, even though I am getting the oldest writing partner ever, to work on a book that nobody will want to read.

CHAPTER 10: FOUNTAIN SQUARE

Frank and I meet the next day in an activity room, to begin work on the story. I normally just ramble on and on and try to create a story later in the editing process, much like a film director might in movie making. Frank has a different process. As I pull out a pen and paper, Frank turns his wheelchair away and heads toward the door. With his cane tip, he flips off the overhead lights.

"I can't work in fluorescents and we need some mood lighting."

"Frank, it's day time. I'm not sure that's going to make a difference."

"Everything makes a difference," he says. With this he rolls his chair forward a couple feet until the sun shining through the window hits his face. Frank found his spotlight, and I realize that I am dealing with quite the storyteller.

Frank begins slowly and very dramatically: "The year was 1937, Franklin Roosevelt was president of the United States, and the country was in the midst of the Great Depression. In Cincinnati, the Great Depression was compounded with the Great Flood, making things not too great at all. The city was literally sliced in thirds for 19 days by water, leaving 20 million dollars worth of damage when it receded. That amount was incomprehensible to people who were scraping by on a dime, many already unemployed. The water reached 21 feet at home plate of Crosley Field down by the river. One of every eight people was left homeless."

"Jesus Frank, you're right, not funny so far. Dad told me about the flood, but he was most excited about the dog sized rats running up the streets to avoid the water."

"Yes, that was the year that the river, which had brought so much trade and wealth to the city, turned on us. Ironic maybe that our story begins at Fountain Square."

"I don't think you know what irony means, Frank"

"Then I don't think *you* know that the Tyler Davidson

Fountain, in the center of town, is a sculptural celebration of the life-enhancing pleasures of water. The flood had royally screwed Cincinnati in the last year, yet we gathered around a fountain celebrating water."

"I stand corrected. You do know what irony means, and I will keep my mouth shut. Please continue, and I will just take notes."

"As I was saying, It was a beautifully cold December evening and the Lambrinides family was walking from their small apartment on 4th and Plum Streets, keeping a quick pace east to Fountain Square. I know this, because I was tagging along with them. Billy and Christy were leading the way to the annual lighting of the Christmas tree, a tradition the whole neighborhood looked forward to. They were followed by seven-year-old Johnny, wearing his flight goggles, which he rarely took off, outdoors or in. Johnny was running to catch his brothers, arms outstretched like wings, but feet not quite getting up enough speed for takeoff. Nicholas and Alexandria smiled their way across town, occasionally steering their youngest flyer in the right direction. We arrived to Fountain Square and Christmas was already in the air. Sleigh bells on horse drawn carriages were ringing and carolers were singing. The great lady towering above us, who normally had water spilling from her palms, suddenly started showering the center of town with hundreds of twinkling lights.

Christy immediately ran off to join the carolers. Christy loved singing and could usually be heard singing along with anything on the radio, but his favorite was The Andrew Sisters. It was adorable, yet odd, to watch a ten-year-old boy trying to sing along with all three of the women's parts at the same time. He would start with LaVerne, switch to Patty, and end as Maxine singing in Yiddish, "Bei Mir Bist Do Schön." He'd been singing Christmas songs since the day after Halloween. Billy had a beautiful voice too, but it was rarely heard alone. He didn't like to be the center of attention, and with a brother ten minutes older who looked just like him, he didn't have to be. He got used to Chris answering for both of them when they were asked questions, and that served him well. Billy was a listener, and when he did chime in it was usually to make somebody laugh.

Nicholas had to leave the celebration early and head to work, so he said his goodbyes and went on his way. He was supposed to be off work from The Emperor that night, but Marty called him in at the last minute to cook."

"Is this skinny Marty Behrens you told me about the other day?" I interrupted. I just realized that I am now interrupting in my own book. How in the hell did this happen?

"The one and only. He was a rich asshole, who didn't care a lick for anybody or anything, other than money. He had a mean little daughter too, named Marylin Behrens. The apple didn't fall far from that tree. I remember her visiting work one day and making fun of another girl's homemade dress. She taunted the girl, asking if her mother had made it out of an old sugar sack. Marylin ended up being a total bitch her whole life, but that's another story."

"Language, Frank, this is a family story. If I can't cuss, neither can you," I interrupted. "Also, times have changed. If you have something hand-stitched today it's not made fun of, it's expensive and called haute couture. Marylin could not afford a sugar sack dress today if she wanted one."

"You can edit out the language if you must, but 'bitch' really describes her best. Continuing, although Nicholas wasn't supposed to be working during the tree-lighting ceremony, Marty called him in at the last minute, so he could bring his own family to the celebration. This was not the first time that Nicholas had to cover for Marty, and his patience was running thin with his boss. Nicholas was a magician in the kitchen but was being held back by the indifference, and the cheapness of Marty. Marty didn't approve of him tampering with the staples on the menu, particularly the bad chili, but he did let him create the specials of the night. Rumors about Nicholas' cooking traveled fast, and the restaurant was busiest when he was in the kitchen. Nicholas pleaded with Marty to let him make changes to the whole menu, but as soon as he mentioned new spices or better quality meats, the conversation would end.

We were enjoying the fountain festivities, when I spotted my older brother in the crowd. Vito was a contract photographer for the Cincinnati Enquirer at the time, and was snapping shots of the merry gatherers and shoppers on the square. He was covering a shift for someone, to make extra holiday money, but as soon as he saw us, he worked his way through the maze of electric candy canes and angels with something to say.

'Hello. Happy holidays! Great night for the fountain lighting isn't it?' Vito exclaimed, out of breath from capturing his shots.

Alexandria said, 'hello' and smiled because she had no idea

what Vito said beyond 'hello.' The neighbors liked each other despite the communication barriers, or perhaps because of them. When she had a willing translator, Alexandria liked to complain in half-truths about how the city paper didn't represent the new immigrants. There weren't a lot of Greeks or Italians in Cincinnati and, therefore, not much news of them in print, but she still teased Vito about this. Billy enjoyed hanging out with Vito and looking at all his photographs of what was going on in other corners of the city. These images fascinated him, and Vito didn't mind the company.

Vito focused his attention on Billy and continued, 'I'm glad I ran into you. My Uncle is coming to stay with us for the holidays and I'm going to pick him up at Union Terminal tomorrow. I know how much you like the trains and thought you might want to come along with Frank and I for the ride.'

'Thanks, Vito. Wow, that will be great. Can I ride in the front seat of your car too?' Billy was as excited about the car ride as he was about seeing all the trains at the station. I always got to ride around in the car, so it was less of a thrill for me, but I was looking forward to seeing my uncle. I couldn't remember meeting him before, although my parents assured me I had. I was just too young to remember. I could tell everyone liked him, and my parents, Maria and Joe, were busy prepping the house for his arrival.

'You can ride in the front on the way over, but you'll have to fight my uncle for the front on the way home. I'll come get you after noon, but you have to ask your mom if it's okay first.'

Billy asked his mother in Greek, and she nodded and said 'thank you' to Vito. Billy could have asked her anything to get her to nod 'yes,' but he knew she wouldn't mind this, so he actually translated the question correctly.

My brother walked us back to the apartment building on Plum Street, stopping to take some pictures along the way. The city was truly in a state of rebirth since the floods, and he liked to document it's progress on film. He took a photograph of the Shillito's department store all decked out for the holidays, with it's glistening new limestone, half-way covering it's flood-scarred brick. This gave us time to watch the mechanical bears and penguins dance around the toys in the kaleidoscope windows. We knew that's as close as we would get to most of the merchandise that year, but didn't care. We were happy, and Santa had never let us down before."

Frank's words got slower, "So, that's how the story begins. It's Christmas time in Cincinnati, Ohio, and my Uncle Bob is coming for a visit."

"Wow, Frank, I'm really surprised. The story is more about my family than I expected, and it sounds like you've told it before."

"Well, of course I've told it before, you don't think this is just off the cuff do you? Stories evolve, and they change, depending on who my audience is. I've never told it to a Lambrinides before, but it's time. You'll come to see that it's also about your family business, but I don't want to get too far ahead of myself."

"Honestly Frank, it's a little more finished than I expected, there's too much exposition, and it's a bit long-winded with all the dialogue. How in the hell do you remember what people said?"

"I've been telling the story for years and the more I tell it, the more permanent it becomes in my mind. This is how the events unfolded, so if you don't like it, we can just stop right now."

"No, I like it a lot." It's a story about my family that I've never heard, containing relatives and neighbors I've never met. How could I not enjoy it?

I did have one question I had to ask. "Frank, is this whole story about 10-year-olds? I don't like kids; particularly cute, snarky ones."

"The story is what it is. If it would make you feel better, I would say half is about adults that have not hit puberty yet."

Oh God, I am writing a Christmas story involving children. I am now making the fart smelling, pucker-face myself. Even I'm not going to read my book. Maybe I can write the kid characters out later. Is it wrong to remove your father from a story about his life?

CHAPTER 11: UNION TERMINAL

The next morning mom and I visit with dad at the nursing home, and he is excited because he is getting released that afternoon. He has apparently been up and ready since the crack of dawn. He is less than excited that they are teaching him to walk with a cane for stability.

"Dad, you are getting around great. Who cares if you have a cane, or a walker, or whatever helps you stay mobile?"

"It makes me feel old," he responds, this time sounding depressed.

"Are you sure it's not being 80 that is making you feel old?" I realize I sound like a dick, but I don't want to baby my dad, and sarcasm has always served us well. "Dad, your age is your age. You can be a young, happy 80, getting around with a cane, or you can be a depressed 80, sitting in a rocking chair doing nothing. Luckily, right now, it's your choice."

"This is more bullshit, and getting old stinks."

"Yes, on both counts." I say with a smile. It's fun to share the banal realities of existence with your parents. There was a time when they shielded me from anything that was bad about life, death to be specific, but now we're all on the sinking ship together.

Nurses and attendants, who have quickly grown attached to dad, come into the room to say their goodbyes. As they give him big hugs, dad just looks at me and rolls his eyes. He doesn't like being touched by the strangers, and just wants to leave. Mom is mortified by dad's blatant eye communication, so keeps yelling, "Bill. Bill!" So now, the nurses are also aware of the eye rolling, if they weren't before.

Dad has one final therapy session before he gets checked out of the spa-like, luxury accommodations. Yes, again, sarcasm. I find Frank in the activity room, this time with four other seniors in wheel chairs gathered around him. He is telling them the same story he began with me the other day.

"Hi Frank. I see you have a crowd with you this afternoon."

"I'm popular," he says proudly. "They asked me what we were talking about the other day and I explained that I knew a story about your family. They want to hear it too. How's your dad doing by the way?"

"Well, good and bad. He's excited to be going home, but he hates using the cane they just gave him."

Franks bursts out laughing, and with it comes a spray of graham crackers.

"Real nice, Frank, lots of love and support from you."

"I'm sorry," Frank says still laughing, "I'm just surprised he has any issues with a cane, and you will soon see why. I'm really happy he gets to go home though. What about the story?"

"What about it? I'm here now, and I'll still be bringing dad back for more therapy. We're just changing the name from 'rehabilitation' to 'personal training' for his return visits."

"I was just setting the tone with our new audience. I told them about the tree-lighting ceremony, and I was about to pick-up where we left off."

"Go for it, Frank."

Frank continues his story as dramatically as he did the day before. This time he adds bad fake accents and character voices, which cracks me up.

"The next morning I was down at the Lambrinides' house playing with Billy. The family was starting the day as they often did, with breakfast and the newspaper. The paper was even more significant than the radio to the Lambrinides' because Nicholas could read aloud and translate in Greek for his wife. He would do this for highlights on the radio too, but when he was speaking to her, he often wouldn't be able to hear the next thing being said. The newspaper allowed them to go at their own pace. With the boys selling newspapers on the streets to help make ends meet, there was always one around. In fact, the apartment was being trimmed for Christmas with red-painted newspaper chains and gold paper stars.

Alexandria was buttering a slice of homemade bread for Johnny while Nicholas drank his coffee and read her the latest goings on. She had baked two, one pound loaves the day before, like she did every Saturday, so it was still fresh and fragrant with yeast. Alexandria was always feisty, but she hadn't been herself lately. Your yaya was a very brave woman, brave like most immigrants who picked up and left all they knew to find a better life in America. She, like her husband, left one of the oldest civilizations to join one of the youngest. She escaped poverty and, now, didn't have much more money than she had before, but had something better — hope. What she was missing was a connection with the community. Cincinnati was comprised almost entirely of Germans and a few other European nationalities, with Jewish, Italian, and Greek immigrants just moving in. The language barrier was isolating her, making her lonely and invisible.

Nicholas continued translating the headlines, 'Al Capone was sentenced to 11 years in prison.'

'I didn't like that booze selling tax evader, and I'm happy they caught him. I'm glad he's Italian and not Greek, but what are all the Greeks doing? Hiding under rocks? I challenge you to find a Sedaris, Stergiopolis, or any Greek name that ends in 'acacas' in that paper.

Billy translated this to me in English, adding, 'Nothing

personal Frank. Your family isn't part of the mob.'

We continued with our English to Greek and back to English translations, like a game of telephone. Nicholas read ahead in the paper, 'The verdict finally came in on Arsenic Anna too. I can't believe it took the jury three weeks to decide she was guilty, when the bodies of eight of her elderly gentleman friends were found dead from poison.'

'Are you making me feel better or giving me ideas?' Alexandria laughed, 'What's your point, when she isn't Greek either?'

'She's a German. Well, aren't you glad it's not a Greek doing the killing?'

The conversation moved on from Germans to the insufferable Adolph Hitler, and continued to cover every topic in *The Enquirer*. The family spent the rest of the morning decking the halls, and Billy kept his eye on the clock, which seemed to be ticking curiously slow. We were ready for our adventure and had enough of Christy singing 'Silent Night.' Christy and Billy would be serving as alter boys for mass on Christmas Eve, and Monsignor Anthony chose Christy to sing the solo. He had been loudly practicing for a week, and the entire building must have learned every word of the song already, even the verses in German. I was thrilled when Christy started singing along with the radio to Bessie Smith's 'Gimme a Pig Foot and a Bottle of Beer,' because that song always made me smile. Smith died in a car accident in September of that year, so the radio had been playing a lot of the rich contralto's slow blues. I could understand the beer, but what was she going to do with the pig foot? I was wondering if she was going to eat it or if they were lucky, like a rabbit's foot, when Vito came by to pick us up."

"Frank, pickled pigs feet? I don't mean to interrupt, but I'm still not sure what this story is about."

"Why would I have to tell it to you, if you already knew? You remember weird things when you're old, depending on what circuits are firing off in the noggin. May I continue, or do you just want me to cut to the end and spoil it for everyone? Let's ask one of our new friends who is joining us today."

With this, Frank looked over to the four senior citizens in wheel chairs around him. Two looked at him encouragingly and asked him to continue, one man had fallen fast asleep, and the last said, "cut to the end and spoil it."

"Well Frank, if the sleeping man doesn't get to vote, you should continue. If his falling asleep counts as a vote, then that would make it a tie. Either way, let's pick up the pace, or none of us will live to hear the conflict, let alone the resolution."

"Look at you, using your little writer terms. Your generation only has the patience for soundbites, but I'm sorry, that is not how I tell a story. I shall continue, using fewer adjectives to speed it up."

Frank takes a dramatic pause, a deep inhale, a loud exhale and continues, "Billy was bouncing in the passenger seat of Vito's Plymouth telling him about his different learning units in school when we pulled into Union Terminal. That building never fails to amaze me. It's as if a massive, ten-story tall radio carved of limestone and glass pushed it's way up out of the earth. Just the night before, I had stared at my own radio listening to Buck Rogers in the 25th Century...sponsored by Popsicle, Fudgsicle, and Creamsicle, those delicious frozen confections on a stick, and now it was like I was walking into that radio. The art deco facade was beautiful and, even better, the station was filled with trains. Billy hurried Vito and I inside to show us one of his favorite tricks, unique to the acoustics of the structure.

'Okay. You both stand all the way on the other side of the building under the big arch, and put your ear in the corner by the wall. I'm gonna stand here under this side of the arch and whisper something. You have to guess what I'm saying.'

Vito and I walked about a hundred feet to the other side and stuck our ears against the limestone. Sure enough, clear as can be, we could hear Billy whisper, 'Buy me a Hershey bar.'

Vito laughed and whispered back, 'Didn't your mother teach you manners? What do you say?'

'With almonds,' Billy replied, paused, and followed with an extended, 'Pleeease.'

Vito walked back to Billy laughing, 'I think your trick deserves some chocolate. Come with me, you little con-artist, and then we'll meet the train.'

The train arrived in a cloud of steam, and a parade of merry visitors started filing past. Men and women dressed in their traveling finest, carrying brightly wrapped packages and suitcases from everywhere. In the middle of the bustle stood an old man with a bright white beard and mustache and a big round belly. He smiled a big jolly smile at Vito and walked right toward us.

Billy blurted out 'Holy cow. Cars, trains, and now Santa Claus! My brothers are going to be so jealous,' and then the questions started pouring, 'Your uncle is Santa Claus? Does that make you two elves of some sort? Why didn't he fly here with the magic dust stuff?'

Vito and I exchanged hugs with our uncle. It had been years since we had seen each other, so it was quite the reunion and, for me, introduction. Even Vito was surprised to see our uncle's reddish-beard had turned white and his stomach had grown.

'Billy, meet my favorite uncle, Bob Nicoloro.'

Billy stood silent with his mouth hanging open, and a small dribble of chocolate spit fell out.

'Hello Billy, very nice to make your acquaintance. I will not ask what brown thing you were eating.'

'Nice to meet you too, Mr. Nicoloro,' he replied, and then looked at Vito and said, 'Are you kidding me with this?'

Vito laughed and explained, 'Uncle Bob, my friend Billy thinks Santa Claus arrived early this year on your train.' Uncle Bob got a big kick out of the situation but told Billy that, if he was indeed Santa, which he wasn't, he would be way too busy for a visit this close to Christmas. Billy liked the old man, but wasn't totally convinced he didn't have a red suit with white fur trim in his bags. As we left, Billy showed my uncle the whispering trick at the entrance of the station; he responded with a loud, 'Ho Ho Ho' just to add to the mystery.

We walked out the doors of Union Terminal and saw that it was snowing. It was the first snow of the season, which made the day even more spectacular.

'I brought the snow with me from up north,' Uncle Bob winked, 'It's Christmas snow, and it travels nicely I think.'"

"Frank, you are shitting me. First you have kids and now you have Santa Claus in this story? It is turning into pure holiday cheese."

"You sound like your father. I just told you it's my Uncle Bob. Uncle Bob was a very good man, with great intentions, but he didn't always make the best choices. Let's put it this way, if he was Santa, he would buy all the kids toys from China, which would eventually poison them with lead-leaching paint."

"I like this Uncle Bob. Now we have a story."

CHAPTER 12: ICE ICE BABY

Dad is back at home, still recovering, but getting around nicely. We have to adjust his heart medicines because of the stomach problems, and take him off of blood thinners altogether. This is not an easy task – no more Cumidin, add something else, take away this or that, and try to find the perfect balance. Dad is optimistic, yet still somewhat fuzzy, about what the hell is going on. After a few days, my sister Debbie and I decide to bring him to the local cineplex for a *Silver Screen Classic*. They show old movies every Monday for two dollars, and the place packs it in with senior citizens who are there for the free soda, popcorn, and cookies, which come with the ticket price. I love classic movies, and old people love free things, so it's really a win win. We arrive a bit late to the theater, and the lights are already down, and it's really crowded, not a seat near an aisle anywhere. So, what do we do to my dad, on his first day out of the house, using his cane? That's right, we push him into strangers in the dark.

"But I can't see!"

"We can't see either. Go. You have to push your way through," Debbie says from behind us.

"My eyes haven't adjusted. How do I know when I'm at an empty seat?" dad asked in a loud whisper.

I whispered loudly back, "Do you hear the people screaming when we step on their feet? Keep going till the screaming stops, and it's likely the seat will be empty."

"Great. Just great," dad responds.

He finds a seat and settles in with his popcorn, which is his only reason for being there. Dad loves popcorn but doesn't have much patience for movies any more. I, on the other hand, could not be happier. You never know what film they're going to show, because the schedule is always wrong. I know this, because I've been to several since, and the movie has never been what I've gone to see. This time, I thought we would be seeing a black and white Orson Welles film, but instead got a 1951 Technicolor musical called *Happy Go Lovely*. I love movie musicals, and this was one I have never seen, starring Vera-Ellen, an actress I adore but have only seen in one film. She was one of the stars of *White Christmas*, not Rosemary Clooney, but the other one. I have watched the long legged beauty play Judy Haynes every Christmas since I was a kid, so I was thrilled to see she found other work after it snowed at the Vermont Inn. Did you know she was the model for the original Barbie Doll? I am filled with useless knowledge just for you. If you've ever seen Vera-Ellen's proportions and eyelashes, you would recognize the original no-waisted, big-breasted doll. *Happy Go Lovely* also stars a very charming and funny David Niven, who keeps making subtle queer comments like "...all this place needs is some flowers and gay drapes!" The movie is supposed to take place in Scotland, although not one person has an accent, so they throw in a random bagpipe parade to make the point clear. It is complete irresistible, escapist, fluff and I needed it. Do not underestimate the power of a dark movie house or a free cookie to make you feel better.

The next day I take dad back to Dan's Place for his first training session as a member of the outside world. While he hasn't been using his cane like he's supposed to, he brings it to therapy so he doesn't get in trouble. I settle dad in with a game of Wii golf, and go looking for Frank, who I find in his room looking out the window. His eyes are half open.

"Are you awake, Frank?"

"Now I am." He turns, smiles and continues, "I was just enjoying the view. Is your dad back?"

"He's downstairs being worked out. How are you doing?"

"Oh, I'm fine. I think I was getting used to your company and didn't even realize it."

"Thanks Frank, I'm enjoying having a writing partner also. I guess we're both surprised."

With this, Frank's eyes opened and lit up from inside. He had a purpose again and didn't want to waste time. "Let's gather our audience from the other day and a few more that have heard the story."

"You told more people this story of yours?"

"Nope, the other four told some people. Your family story is proving quite popular with the older set."

"That's hopeful, but probably because they, like you, have not yet discovered the wonders of the world wide web."

We wheel everyone to our activity room, and Frank picks up the story where we left off.

"Billy and I spent the next few days showing Uncle Bob around town after school. The snow flurries continued to dance in the air but never amounted to any accumulation. While nice to look at, we wanted enough to cover the ground for forts and snowballs. We showed my Uncle Bob, our Santa clone, how we would slide down the cold marble steps of the buildings on a piece of cardboard in lieu of sledding. He must have picked up on our readiness for winter fun and started asking questions about the flood. We weren't sure what he was talking about, and then he asked where in the neighborhood was the last place we saw standing water? 'Where, long after the water receded from the flood, was there still a bit left?' We took him back to the Plum Street apartment and pointed out the alley directly behind the building.

'This is it.' I said, 'The last place I remember seeing water.'

'Perfect, this will be perfect,' Uncle Bob excitedly started waving his hand in the air. I had no idea what he was talking about, but I liked that his eyes started twinkling.

'Why are you asking about the flood? Don't worry, I don't think that's going to happen again.' Billy said, also trying to figure out my uncle's intentions.

'I'm not worried. It's going to be great. You'll see tomorrow.' he said as he ran into the building.

Well, the next morning we did see what he was talking about, but first we heard it.

'Ouch! What in the hell?....HELP!' came screaming from the alley at the crack of dawn, waking everyone in the building up.

We all went running downstairs to see what the commotion was all about. I remember seeing Lillian Fowler sitting on her ass with her dog barking in circles around her. Then I realized that she was sitting on a thick sheet of ice. The entire alley looked like sparkling glass and, aside from the screaming injured woman, it looked spectacular. The adults were helping Lillian up, and we were putting our shoes on as quickly as we could to go for a slide across the alley. Uncle Bob made his way downstairs, apologizing the entire way.

'I am so sorry. I didn't realize people use the back entrance. I had the hose going out here for a couple of hours last night. Are you alright, Lillian?'

'No, I am not all right. I got up early to take Mr. Busters for a walk, and now my backside is killing me, and I think I sprained my ankle. '

'Again, I am so sorry. I wanted to surprise the kids, and I thought I would be the first person awake so I could warn everyone else. Is there anything I can do?'

'Yes, there is actually. You can take Mr. Busters for his walk, because I'm going back upstairs to bed. And you can come back tomorrow morning and take Mr. Busters for another walk, and another the day after that, and so on, until my ankle is better.'

That was the deal as I recall, but we didn't really care about any of that. We had a homemade ice rink, skates, and hockey to play. We glided around that alley every day after school until the sun dipped behind the brick buildings and the cold winds off the river began to blow.

Uncle Bob now had a morning routine, which included dog walking, as well as making nice to Lillian Fowler. He often brought little Johnny along with him for company and would sometimes let him hold the reigns of the giant dog. Eventually Uncle Bob did win over Lillian Fowler, and their morning routine extended to coffee together following Mr. Busters' relief.

Nicholas and Alexandria, had their own agendas at the time, but they weren't sharing them with each other. I know this because they were sharing them with my parents. My mom would tell me how Alexandria was worried about getting all her spices bought and her baking done before Christmas. Spices and nuts were not cheap, and both of the ladies used plates of their baked goods as holiday presents for the neighbors, something they both took great pride in. My father would tell me how Nicholas really wanted to change things at work, he was sick of having to prepare things that weren't up to his standards. Although he practiced and refined his recipes at home, he wanted to be able to experiment with larger, restaurant quantities. He really wanted to fix that chili, and have enough customers taste it to know if it was as good as it could be. To see if the same thing that he loved, would be loved by everyone else.

The weekend before Christmas both families again headed east across town, this time to see the living nativity scene at

Lytle Park. We recognized Mary, Joseph and the wise men because Nick Batsalis had volunteered to make their costumes, so they'd been around Plum Street. They would go into the tailor shop for a fitting and come out glassy-eyed and happy. This was a particularly cold night in Cincinnati, so the shepherds were actually passing around a flask to stay warm."

"Working the manger sounds like a great seasonal job at the time. They got you stoned during the costume fitting and got you drunk during the show," I interrupted.

"I know! Actually, I remember your dad and I laughing hysterically when a wise man started raising his flask in the air and toasting the baby Jesus. Once one of them broke holy character, they all started laughing contagiously."

"I believe that's what the original virgin birth would have looked like; less solemn head bowing, and more liquor and laughter. Hello? She got pregnant by the Lord without sex, traveled miles on a donkey, and finally had the baby in a stable. There definitely would have been some celebrating after that one. 'Whoop! Whoop! Who just birthed the Son of God? I did! Now pass the hooch and something to smoke other than frankincense, because Mary is ready to party.

Also, bring out the little drummer boy to get some beats going too, because there shall be dancing, people.'"

Frank looks seriously at me. "Mary doesn't talk like that."

"My Mary does. How do you know what Mary sounded like? I'm making her more relatable. Jesus himself is usually pictured in the manger with his arms out like he's doing the YMCA dance, so I don't see why Mary wouldn't appreciate some fun."

"Moving on. We stayed at the nativity longer than we planned, because Johnny was strangely riveted. There were no airplanes involved, but something about that manger scene had him transfixed. As we were walking back across town we were all discussing the plans for the week. The men would be working every day and covering a few nights so they could be off on Christmas Saturday, as they had planned with Marty Behrens. The women would spend the week baking their Greek and Italian sweets for gift giving. All of the kids were counting down the last couple days of school before our Christmas break and planning all the snowmen and igloos to be built.

The next morning we woke up to a city covered in glass. It

was beautiful. An ice storm during the night had coated absolutely everything, so buildings and tree branches looked as though they had been sealed in crystal. It was also an unusually sunny morning, so light was dancing off of everything, and icicles were dripping on the sidewalk. After church we headed north to the 6th Street Market between Elm and Central to get cooking and baking supplies for the week. I didn't think that huge, vibrant market would ever disappear, but nothing lasts forever I guess. The Findlay Market is still in business for outdoor market and nostalgia lovers. The women each grabbed a son to be translator and perused the winter vegetables, which were displayed outside in the open section of the market. The men headed inside to inspect the spices and fresh meats. Nicholas ignored the spices that he wanted to purchase to experiment with his chili and focused on the spices that Alexandra would need for her baklava and kourabiethes. He would return and purchase a small amount of beef for Christmas dinner when he had more money.

I remember we were walking home from the market, and mom was talking about baking her sweet, chewy pignoli cookies. Then, in an instant, everything changed. I heard a crack and everything went dark."

With this, Frank stopped. He looked up and the room was silent, and he gave a big smile.

"That would be a good place to end a chapter I think. Everybody likes a little cliff hanger." Frank said and paused.

CHAPTER 13: JOHNNY ANGEL

"Are you serious? You cannot tell me where to start and stop chapters, when I don't even know how long this story is. Oh my God, Frank. What happened?"

"I woke up that night in the hospital with a throbbing headache and my leg wrapped up tightly. An icicle had fallen off the overhang and smacked me right in the head. I don't remember anything, but they told me that it knocked me unconscious, and when I fell down I sprained my ankle."

"Oh my God, I hear about icicles killing people every year, but I never believed I'd actually meet someone that it happened to."

"I'm not dead. I'm still here doing the talking." Frank said.

"I know Frank. Still, you're lucky to be alive." This was like meeting someone that was hit by a tornado without ever visiting a trailer park. What are the odds?

"Lucky, yes, but wrecked. I had always been a sickly child, but with this accident I learned that I have an actual physical disorder. I have slow growing and slow healing muscles and bones, which has had me using canes or a wheel chair all of my life. As bad as that sounds, that's not what I was upset about at the time. I was worried about what people would think. At the time, a child walking with canes often meant they had something infectious, like polio, and I wasn't ready for all that fear and pity."

"Wow, Frank. I am so sorry. I don't want to make light of the situation, but you are totally the Tiny Tim of this story."

"First of all, I'm neither Tiny nor Tim. Secondly, Tiny Tim's character is pivotal, because whether he lives or dies depends upon the actions of Scrooge. I have to live, because I'm the narrator."

"Don't you tell me who has to live or die in my book, Tiny Frank. I still can't believe that I haven't heard any of this before."

"The events had a big impact on my life. I remember recovering that week in the upstairs apartment and relying on people for everything because I couldn't get around. I was learning to use a cane, which I despised, and your dad would come visit and give me encouragement. I was feeling sorry for myself, and dreading Christmas for the first time. I didn't want to show up at midnight mass on Friday using a cane like a disabled person. I had already learned that kids could be cruel if you were different, and I was different enough before the accident. What I didn't know is that when your dad wasn't visiting me, he was busy planning something with the neighborhood kids for that mass.

The Wednesday before Christmas, my dad and Nicholas were finishing their shift at The Emperor, when Marty Behrens dropped the final bomb on them. He told them they were going to have to work on Christmas Day. The men had asked for the day off months in advance, so this news came as a big surprise.'

'Don't take this personally, it's just business and I am going to keep the restaurant open. We are closed the next day on Sunday anyway, so why don't you just celebrate with your families then?' Marty suggested.

Nicholas, who is always calm, started raising his voice, 'Marty, you approved this day off long ago, and we shouldn't have needed to even ask, because it's a national holiday. Christmas is on Saturday this year, not Sunday.'

'There are plenty of people in town that would love to have a job this Christmas, if you don't want yours.' Behrens hissed back.

Which was true, and Nicholas knew it. This is why Nicholas didn't continue the argument, but he didn't retreat either. Something snapped inside him at this moment. He knew he couldn't continue working for this horrible man, and it was time to take his skills to the next level. He needed to open his own restaurant. He also needed to play nice with Marty for a little while longer, to keep the cash flowing and to do some more recipe testing.

By Thursday morning our apartment looked and smelled like an Italian pastry shop. Mom had gone to run some errands, and there were trays of biscotti and florentines cooling on racks waiting to be eaten. I looked out the window and saw Johnny walking Mr. Busters. What I didn't see was Uncle Bob following both of them. A half an hour later I was resting my leg and dozed off into a nap, when I was awoken by a loud, barking dog in our kitchen. My heart stopped and I struggled to make my way to the baked goods and the neighbor's beast. It was a complete and total mess. Mr. Busters, now wearing a beard of cannoli crumbs, had eaten dozens of cookies, and the rest were broken to bits. Christmas was officially ruined, and I needed someone to blame. I yelled at the dog but needed someone human to vent my anger at, so started screaming down the stairs at Johnny. I yelled all sorts of terrible things at that kid for not watching the dog. I was in tears and yelled for the longest time. I didn't realize that Johnny wasn't to blame, or that he ran away crying as soon as I started my tirade."

"Real nice Frank, make a little kid cry. Did you kick the dog, too?"

"No, and don't forget that I was a kid also. I was guilty enough when I found out what I'd done. We didn't realize Johnny was gone for a few hours because nobody saw him leaving. Everybody assumed he'd gone with Christy to the church for a rehearsal. So, when Christy returned and didn't have Johnny with him, the whole building went into panic mode. I learned that it was Uncle Bob who had left our apartment door open and let Mr. Busters get loose. I explained the miscommunication to everyone, and that I was probably responsible for Johnny disappearing. I was petrified that something bad was going to happen and it would be my fault.

Everyone went looking for Johnny, and I mean everyone. Word spread quickly, and all the neighbors joined the search. For the rest of the afternoon and into the evening I could hear people screaming his name across town. 'Johnny! Johnny!', but never a response. It got dark and the search became even more desperate. It was the night before Christmas Eve, so we couldn't just go around screaming at the top of our lungs, disturbing all the neighbors. So the plan was made to go from screaming to singing. Johnny loved to listen to Christy, so they decided to have him lead the group in carols as loud as he could. Billy and I waited back at the apartment in case Johnny returned home on his own, and the rest of the group went searching. Christy walked and sang for hours, never once feeling his legs or voice grow tired. The group sang every song they could think of, diligently combing every block, getting further and further away from the house. They searched late into the night, but it wasn't until Christy began singing 'Away in a Manger' that something jogged his memory, and they headed east. Sure enough, there in the living nativity scene at Lytle Park was a very short angel wearing wings and flight goggles, buzzing in circles around the crib like a crop duster. A few of the men working at the display recognized Johnny from the week before and were keeping him occupied until they were done and could bring him home safely. I was never so happy as when everyone returned to Plum Street celebrating their find."

I could tell from the look on his face that Frank is still relieved they had found the boy. I could also tell that he was getting tired, and I had to pick up dad from therapy, so we ended our story session.

That night we go out to dinner with the whole family, to a place that features a live band playing to a hopping dance floor. What first surprises me is that the room is filled with black people and white people partying together in harmony. In California, this is the norm, but in racially divided Cincinnati, this is an unusual and pleasant sight to behold. I tell this to my sister and her deadpan response is "Yeah I know. We hate the Mexicans now." She's kidding, mind you, and I have never even seen a Mexican in Ohio, which is odd. The second thing I notice is that there are a shocking amount of little people at the restaurant. Really short people make me very uncomfortable, and they tend to seek me out. They smell fear, so I assume fear-smell must be emitted from some place low on our bodies, maybe our feet. My mother, in contrast, is obsessed with the tiny. She's addicted to a reality show called "Little People," and shares all their adventures with me.

"Oh my God, they're so cute, you must watch! You get to see them climbing the shelves at the grocery store and going to parties to meet other little people. They don't keep a very tidy house, though."

Well, at least not the top half of the house. Yuck. I don't want to think about tiny feet climbing all over the shelves at the Ralph's. My mother had a twinkle in her eye that night. I know she was hoping the vertically challenged would start doing some dance of the dwarfs after a few rounds of margaritas, and she might get to pick one up if they happened to fall. This, combined with the overabundance of elves on television during the holiday, has my mom in Little People heaven and me nearly hyperventilating. On a side note, did you know you can't call them 'midgets' anymore or they will kick your ass? Oh, and I'm not sure if I can discuss whites and blacks, either. I believe it would have been more politically correct to have said, 'caucasians' and 'chocolate brothers.'

CHAPTER 14: A CANDY CANE

The next morning I come downstairs to find my parents finishing breakfast at the kitchen island. We say our good mornings and I pour myself a cup of coffee, grab a spoonful of sugar out of the canister and drop it into the hot Folgers. It starts to bubble and fizz, creating an acid colored foam on top, like the worst latte ever. This should not happen. I am still in the waking process, so I double check that I chose the canister labeled 'Sugar' and not the one labeled 'Arsenic.'

"Oh my God! Mom, what the hell did I just put in my coffee, that the coffee clearly didn't like?"

"It's artificial sweetener."

"Um, gross. You were always a pink packet, saccharin lady. I know that stuff is toxic enough to cause cancer in laboratory rats, but I don't recall a chemical reaction in the mug."

"It's got fiber now," she responds matter-of-factly.

"Good Lord, eat an apple or something." Is it alright that it looks like the sweetener was poured out of someone's sinister poison ring, as long as it keeps you regular? I don't think so. I take a taste, for kicks, just to see if there is any of the same sensation as eating Pop Rocks. There is not, so I pour the chemically sweet, poo-inducing liquid down the drain, and start over from scratch.

I'm giving my mom a lecture about not drinking science projects, and my dad starts to yawn, but it's a weird yawn. It looks fake, like a bad actor's yawn. He repeats this Keanu Reeves-esque yawn again and again, and then says that he's feeling nauseous. My dad stands up to pull a handkerchief out of his pocket and presses it to his mouth, as if to dyke a dam and hold back sickness. I will now interrupt myself to let you know that I think handkerchiefs are disgusting, in that it's acceptable to use them and return them to your pocket for later, when you might need that booger-encrusted rag. I turn around and look for a bucket or bowl for my dad in the kitchen, which I would swear is rearranged between each of my visits. I turn back, holding some piece of useless Tupperware, a deviled egg carrier I think, and my dad starts vomiting and passing out. I see him start to fall in slow motion, and I literally dive across the room to catch his head before it hits the hardwood. He is getting sick while he's unconscious and I'm barking orders at my mom to call 911 and we are all having a total meltdown. I am lying on the floor in a pool of vomit and holding my dad when he comes to and says, "What happened? Who got sick?" Knowing he still has a great sense of humor I respond, "Who do you think? I puked and pushed you down into it, of course." He laughs, and I internally freak out as we wait for the ambulance. And here we are, yet again, discussing another puke incident, in what I should title *My Vomitous Holiday Vacation.*

A team of paramedics enters the house and takes control of the situation. My dad seems to be doing better, but I am worried that he may have broken something when he fell. Old people are always breaking things, so I want to make sure dad doesn't need a new hip, like Liza. They put dad into the back of the ambulance, and I jump into the front next to the driver and try to pretend none of this is happening. There is a woman's voice on the radio dispatch keeping everything moving, and I'm listening to the medical interrogation of my father going on in the back.

"How old are you sir?"

"I'm 70." he responds.

"You're 81!" I scream to the back. Oh my God, we've lost 11 years. I'm fine with this as long as I get to be 28 again but I don't think it works that way. Plus, I look like shit for 28, so this will not do. He's 81, like it or not.

We arrive at the emergency hospital entrance, and I jump out of the ambulance and run to the back. They open the doors and my dad is laying in the gurney rolling his eyes. My dad has no subtlety with his eye rolling, and I immediately start laughing because I know he's feeling like himself again. He's annoyed by all of the proceedings.

Throughout the ordeal I want to be helpful, but it's my dad that keeps me laughing. At one point we're waiting endlessly in the ER for results of a CAT scan that my dad has already forgotten he had. He gets impatient and starts with, "What are we waiting for? When can we get out of here?" I respond slowly to him, hoping the words are sinking in, "Dad, we have to wait for the test results. We have to make sure you didn't have a stroke when you passed out." With this my dad makes a full on stroke-face and says, "What, like this?" He closes one eye and continues to talk out of the side of his mouth, like Quasimodo.

We continue to laugh through the IVs, which he pulls out, through the monitoring which shows his heart making drastic pauses, and through all of the hospital crap. The good news is there were no strokes, except for my father's limited improvisations, and the better news is that he is back home a few days later.

A week passes before we head back to the nursing home for more rehabilitation and a visit with Frank. I find him watching a huge birdcage in one of the lounges we haven't spent time in yet. I hate birds, but I don't say this.

"This is nice Frank, although the squawking might distract from the rest of your story."

"Nice? I think it's depressing, like some sort of parrot prison. I mean, they have beautiful wings, just ready to soar them into the clouds if they could just make it past the bars. Let's get the hell out of here and gather the group. I was worried that you thought the story was over because we had found

Johnny."

"Nope, dad gave us a scare and had to go back to the hospital for a few days. He's doing great now though."

Frank walks over to a huge room with bingo already in process. He makes his way through the wheelchairs to the front and whispers in the ear of the man calling numbers, who looks a bit confused. The man continues to call numbers, until an old woman on oxygen, with a gigantic pink bow in her hair, wheezes that she won. At this point Frank just grabs the microphone and takes over.

"Congratulations Betty, come get your cookie. That will be the final game for the day, because I'm about to finish the story. I know that news travels around here faster than we can even move somehow, and I don't want you to hear some watered-down version of the finale, so I'm holding you all hostage here."

Oh dear God, there is a hostage situation at the senior center, and I am involved. Not to mention the fact that everyone in the room is wearing adult diapers, so we're not even going to get bathroom breaks for a chance to escape.

"I woke up Christmas Eve morning, relieved that Johnny had

been found the night before. I still had to deal with the fact that I was going to show up at mass that night walking with a cane. Most of the kids from school would be there, so I was sure to be even more ostracized than I had been in the past. I wasn't the only one worried about the church service that night; Billy was in shock all day long. You see, after all the yelling and singing for Johnny the night before, Christy woke up voiceless. His throat was red and raw, and literally not a sound was coming out. Alexandria was still hopeful that it would heal, but was now looking at Billy as a backup solution to the problem at hand. If one twin was broken, use the other. Billy had never sung in front of anyone, and didn't want to start that night, but he also wasn't about to disappoint his parents, after all they'd been through the night before. He knew the song by heart from hearing Christy sing it on a constant loop, but he spent the day seeing if he could make the same sounds come out of his own mouth.

There was still another matter unresolved, and that was what was to be done about Christmas dinner the next day with the men having to work. Alexandria had already decided that she would rather the family be together, even if it wasn't at home, so she planned to spend the day at The Emperor with her husband and boys. My family concurred, so we all would be spending our holiday at a downtown greasy spoon together. Nicholas realized that with Marty at home for the holiday, he could do whatever he wanted with the menu that day. He could actually make recipes that *he* wanted to make, and have a group of customers to sample his goods. He also needed to make something delicious that could feed both families for Christmas, with enough to share with willing customers. Both families put their meager savings together for their holiday meal and left it in the able hands of Nicholas, who immediately left for the Central Market.

The whole way there Nicholas thought of what he wanted to make, but the traditional meals didn't feel right to him. He knew he didn't have the budget to do a large roast beef with all the trimmings, and the families had just had turkey and stuffing the month before. He also kept thinking about the horrible chili that Marty served. He thought about the efficiency of serving a large group out of one pot, if what was in the pot was actually delicious. He was going to make his own chili, but with a twist.

Once he got to the market and started pricing items, he was still coming up short. He perused the spices and picked up a few, but suddenly remembered the spices that Alexandria had purchased for her cookies. He was sure she still had some left he could use, and this started him thinking about some Greek dishes that share the same spices. Moussaka uses ground lamb with a blend of tomatoes, onions, and cinnamon, layered over eggplant and topped with custard sauce and cheese. He bought pounds of the best quality ground beef instead of lamb, and he purchased a huge brick of aged mild cheddar cheese. Eggplant was not a staple at the market, but he needed something to balance out the meat and expand the meal. He thought of another Greek dish that spices meat similarly, with allspice, nutmeg and clove, which his wife had also purchased. Pastitsio has a layer of pasta below its flavored ground beef, and this would work as an excellent model. While the baked dish normally has a bechamel over the top, the melting cheddar would offer the same cooling effect.

Nicholas found inspiration and returned to his kitchen to spend the day over pots of simmering meats and onion. There was chopping and grinding, followed by bubbling sauces under percolating lids, letting off steaming wafts of the sweet and spicy concoction. The smells coming out of the kitchen were like nothing I had ever experienced before.

That night both families put on their best clothes and walked together to St Peter in Chains Cathedral. Billy and Christy left early, because they would be serving mass with Monsignor Anthony, one of them singing the solo. I can now tell you that Christy never got his voice back that day. It was all up to Billy."

"You are shitting me!" I blurt out. The entire room turns and gives me the evil eye, several of them shushing me. Seniors do not like story time interrupted. I will just be quiet now and let the old man finish.

"It was a cold, slow walk to West 8th Street and I was in no hurry to get there. My leg had stopped hurting, but the cane I had to use made me look weak. I was imagining everyone staring and whispering about the poor boy with polio. All I wanted for Christmas was to be a normal kid, and I knew that was no longer possible. Or at least, I *thought* that was no longer possible.

We pushed open the big wooden doors, and the smell of incense and evergreens hit my nose. I had my head lowered but could tell the room was already packed with families. I looked up to see a boy about my age standing with a cane. I was completely confused. I took a few more steps and noticed the boy in front of him had a large stick he was walking with, and so did his younger brother. The girl next to them had a cane also. I saw a few of the kids from school, and they all had canes of some sort. It was wonderful. Some had yardsticks, some had umbrellas, but they all carried something. I walked up the center aisle with my family, and got a smile or a nod from each and every person I passed. They all knew. I didn't have to explain anything, because someone already had. They all knew, and nobody cared at all. Well, that's not exactly correct. They didn't care about my condition, but they did care about me. In fact, they cared enough about me to go out of their way to make me feel normal, to feel accepted.

The mass began, and it was the most beautiful service I can remember. I was still floating on the reception I'd received from my friends as I walked in with my newly fantastic cane. Billy and Christy looked like matching bookends at the altar, both of them a bit nervous about the solo to be sung. Then when the time came for Christy to sing, and without anybody knowing, Billy stood up. He opened his hymnal, the organ began to play, and he sang. Quiet at first, then louder and louder, until he was filling that cathedral with his voice. 'Silent Night' has never sounded so good to me, and Nicholas and Alexandria were beaming with pride. I noticed Uncle Bob and Mrs. Fowler moving about with Vito in the back of church, shooting pictures.

That Christmas morning it started to snow. A light, dancing snow, where the flakes float in every direction, not just down. Each of the families opened the gifts that Santa had dropped at their respective apartments. Nicholas and my dad headed to The Emperor shortly after the presents had been opened to make the final preparations for the holiday feast. We followed a couple hours later, with mom and Alexandria handing out plates of Greek and the remaining Italian cookies to neighbors on the way. Nobody can hide their excitement when they're handed a plate of baklava. What's not to like about layers of nuts and phyllo dough soaked in sticky, sweet syrup?

We walk into The Emperor and immediately notice that it smells different than it ever has, something has already permeated the air. The smell alone causes my mouth to water, which is strange, because my nose can't possibly know what my mouth has in store for it yet. Nicholas is beaming, and I'm not sure if he's still beaming from his son's performance the night before or if it's something else entirely. Tables had been pushed together to make one long table down the middle of the restaurant, and we all take seats. It's initially just our families, but any customers that arrive are introduced and seated at the group table as well. Nicholas and my dad ask each of us if we like onions and if we like beans, make notes on a piece of paper and then return to the open grill area, where I can see a huge pot of meat sauce bubbling on the stove. Next to that pot is a pot of hot spaghetti, which my dad begins dishing out on plates. He hands the steaming plates of pasta to Nicholas, who ladles the rich, dark chili sauce over the noodles, and tops this with either warm kidney beans, cool diced onions, or both. The entire plate is mounded high with grated cheddar, a mountain of yellow cheese, gooey and melting around the edges. The plates are quickly assembled and served around the table, and Nicholas pours wine he had smuggled into the diner for the adults, and makes a toast.

'It's been a tough year for all of us, one I will never forget. The fact that we are all here together is enough to be celebrating, but we have much more than that, much more than most. We have family and a community of friends and loved ones that are watching out for us. Thank you God for this family in Cincinnati and for providing this meal. I hope you all enjoy it.'

Nicholas specifically looks at my family and laughing says, 'Now, I know you Italians like to twirl your pasta, but this is a Greek dish, and it should be cut with your fork. I want you to get a bit of each of the layers in every bite.' With this, we all take our forks and cut into our plates of hot chili and spaghetti and melting cheese. There is silence, other than the radio playing Christmas tunes, as we take our first bites of this very unconventional holiday dinner.

It was unlike anything I or anybody else at that table had tasted before. Absolutely delicious. It tasted like Christmas. The savory meat combined with the sweet cinnamon and nutmeg teased my tongue. We didn't know until years later that we were the first people to ever taste what would become known as Skyline Chili. It would take over 10 years for Nicholas to iron out the details and save the money needed to open his own place, but the famous secret recipe was ready. We all knew we were eating something special that afternoon. You could taste the magic and the love put into it.

We were finishing our meal, when Uncle Bob came strolling into the restaurant with Mrs. Fowler and her daughter, along with Vito, wearing a big, dopey grin on his face. He looked like he was up to something.

Vito could keep his secret no longer. 'Well, I would have

thought one of these paperboys would be working on Christmas, but I guess I have to deliver the good news today. How about I trade you one of the newspapers I have in my hand for a few plates of whatever smells so good that you're eating?' With that Vito tossed a copy of the paper on the middle of the table. There, on the front of *The Cincinnati Enquirer*, was a full-page picture of Billy singing at church with a headline reading GLORY TO GOD IN THE HIGHEST....ON EARTH PEACE, GOOD WILL TOWARD MEN. Just the little Greek boy, standing alone in front of a beautiful stone angel and looking up toward the heavens, a perfect representation of Christmas in Cincinnati. Alexandria began to cry, and then to laugh, and then to cry. Nicholas looked at all the people surrounding his makeshift table; thought of all the people that helped search for his boy just nights before. The bond between a family and a city was formed. When Nicholas looked out the window of The Emperor he was surrounded by the buildings that made up that city's beautiful skyline. He made a note to some day honor those buildings of people, working to make things better.

And that, my friends, is the story of Plum Street and the birth of a Cincinnati institution, Skyline Chili."

The room bursts into applause. I am overwhelmed. Overwhelmed by not only this story, which I should have heard before, but overwhelmed by the reaction of the others hearing it. The story doesn't just belong to my family, but like Skyline Chili, it belongs to everyone that is proud to call Cincinnati, Ohio home. There are now over 150 Skyline Chili restaurants in Ohio, Indiana, Kentucky, and as far south as Florida. This story belongs to anyone that is reaching for the American dream, and looking for inspiration to know that dream is alive and well, and it tastes delicious.

"Frank, I'm speechless. Dad made the front page, huh? Thank you for telling me the story. I still find the idea of dad singing suspect, but I have no reason to not believe you. I really don't understand why dad never told me this."

"Are you kidding? Your father would never tell this story, because it makes him look good, and he was never one to toot his own horn. I didn't find out until after the fact that he was the one that had arranged for all the kids to bring canes to church. Project Candy Cane, as it was called around town, was all his idea. I was sure you had already heard about the origins of the chili, but I guess not."

"No, in fact, I heard the same story as everyone else. Just the one that said the name 'Skyline' came from the view of the city from outside of the kitchen window of the original restaurant in Price Hill. I worked in that restaurant as kid. The kitchen didn't face the skyline and there was no view of the city from any window in the place. Your story actually makes more sense."

"The truth doesn't always make the most sense, but at least it's the truth, and that's a start."

CHAPTER 15: HOME

I spend the next few days making final preparations and early celebrations for the holiday. This includes visiting with old friends, like Trisha and Kevin, who now live back in Cincinnati with their daughter Mayson, not far from where we grew up. They have a Christmas tree I love, that looks like it might have been decorated by Dr. Seuss. I am also back and forth on the phone with Albert, who is attending to his grandma in Nevada.

Christmas Eve holds all of the usual Lambrinides family traditions, most of which are about making the group laugh at each other's expense. After dinner and heavy alcohol consumption, we have a piñata for the kids downstairs in the basement. No, we're not Mexican, but it's fun to hit things with sticks. This year's piñata looks like a treasure chest, which isn't very holiday, but the kids are into pirates. Years ago my mother chose a purple dinosaur for the piñata, because my nephew, TJ, was obsessed with Barney. We all realized her mistake as we listened to TJ screaming bloody murder, watching the other kids beating his beloved friend to a pulp with a bat. I was particularly fond of that holiday dinosaur slaying, but fear it may have scarred TJ permanently.

Following this, we sing the "12 Days of Christmas", each person singing and acting out a particular gift. In the name of family fun and embarrassment, I belt out "eight maids a milking" while simulating my best udder-pull. I also catch my niece giving what appears to be a blowjob as a piper piping. If that's not enough, we make the nieces and nephews parade through the house carrying figurines from the nativity scene while singing "Silent Night" before they can open presents. They fight over what character they get to be, and we yell things like "move that ass" to the donkey carrier. These activities are all hurdles my mother creates for us to jump over before getting gifts. With all the singing, you would think we were Mormon, like The Osmonds. Let me assure you, we do not normally hang out and sing songs, although there are the occasional lip-synching performances and talent shows.

The little ones start pulling the brightly wrapped boxes out from under the tree and passing them around. I should now tell you that mom and dad's house is almost entirely deep purple and emerald green, as are many of the packages, because she likes things to match. I look at dad and am reminded that I have this story, this secret that I want to reveal to everyone, but decide to wait and sort it out and write it down, to try to tell it as dramatically as Frank did.

In the middle of opening presents I get a phone call from Albert. "Fanny died today," he said. Everything stops. My first reaction is, "You must have been bad this year, I got a digital camera for Christmas. Santa didn't kill my grandma." I did not say this. Albert has a great sense of humor, but I know the joke is way too soon. "I'm so sorry, baby." is the only thing I can say. "I actually watched her go." he continues, and tells me how he was the only one in the room when she took her last breaths. I console him the best I can, but have to cut the conversation short because my family is waiting for me to continue the festivities. I return to my place on the couch where the unwrapping of the gifts is taking place, sit down and start to cry in the middle of everything. I stand up and quietly remove myself from the room, realizing that my sobbing is seriously making Christmas suck for everyone.

My sister Sherry follows me out and just starts hugging me. It's exactly what I need. "I don't know why I'm crying. I didn't even know her very well." I say through my tears.

"You're crying because Albert's broken, and you can feel it." She is right, I'm crying for Albert. I am actually feeling what he is feeling halfway across the country, which is a strange combination of sorrow and wonder. Sad, because he lost a special person in his life but happy that he was there to say goodbye. Even though this is not an uncommon occurrence, I think it's amazing that this old woman waited for her grandson to come home so she could say goodbye. We have more control over our physical bodies than we know, and I am overwhelmed by the power of the human spirit. It's then that I realize that Albert was given a very special gift for the holiday.

Christmas day I continue on my emotional rollercoaster, now fueled with more sad stories from Albert and surrounded by the entire extended family. My cousin Sandy and I are talking, while she is chasing her new twins around the room.

"I am exhausted now that the babies are crawling. Our manger scene has an earless donkey and a headless wise man from one of the babies attacking it, like Godzilla. Hey, did your mom make you sing songs before getting your gifts last night?" she asks laughing.

"Yep, just like every other Christmas past, except this year I thought it would be swell to cry the entire night. I don't think it went over very well. You know, I actually think it makes perfect sense to have a headless wise man."

"I am so sorry to hear about Albert's grandma, please give him my condolences. You're right about the wise man. I actually found the head but maybe I won't glue it back on. The donkey ear is lost and the twins put everything in their mouths, so it's probably gone for good."

Thinking about Albert's grandma makes me think about my grandparents, and I now realize that I'm crying again. The holiday lights look really pretty through my tears but, seriously, in the voice of Cher, I have got to snap out of it. I dare you to try sharing tales of crossing-over after a little wine while listening to a Carpenter's Christmas album and not cry. Impossible.

My Aunt Mary pulls me aside and tries to make me feel better. She lost her husband to cancer years ago around the holidays. "You know what the nurse told me when Uncle John Died? She said that God brings his favorite children home for Christmas."

She did make me feel better, although this sounded like the tag line to a religious slasher movie to me. I'm now picturing God with a scary clown grin holding a bloody knife in front of the title, "Holiday Horror: God brings his favorite children home for Christmas." Well, I'm freaked out now, but at least I'm not crying under the mistletoe anymore.

The day after Christmas, even though dad doesn't have therapy, I decide to pay a visit to the nursing home to wish Frank a happy holiday and bring him some Skyline chili, of course. Frank's bed is made when I enter his room, so I begin looking for him in all the recreation areas. I get nods and smiles from all my new and very old friends as I pass. When I enter the room with the giant birdcage, I stop. Someone has left the cage open and there are birds flying everywhere in the room. There is a window cracked to the outside, with cold air blowing the open curtains into the room. A bright red bird is standing outside on the ledge. I don't know of birds, so I don't know how else to describe it other than small, and bright red, which I already mentioned. It looked bird-like, nodding its tiny head as if it was questioning the freezing temperatures of freedom. My brain starts clicking— click, click, click; I start to panic and I run. I run to the nurses' station and ask about Frank

"I am so sorry honey, Frank passed away last night in his sleep." I stop and expect everything else to stop also. "You must be Billy."

"Yes, I am, but how did you guess that?"

"Mr. Salamone left you something. Let me find it here."

The nurse opens a file and hands me an envelope with my name on it. Inside is an old faded clipping of newspaper that had been folded in quarters. I gently open it up and its *The Cincinnati Enquirer* dated Saturday Morning, December 25, 1937, and I see the picture of my dad in his serving clothes.

There is a note that says, "To Billy, Vito came to see me last night, so I think our writing time is coming to an end. Make the story yours."

You guessed it, I start to cry again, but there's not much left to come out. I'll have to hydrate before I get any more bad news. I had made and lost a new friend in a very short time, so I suppose the mourning time should be brief also, but I'm doubtful it's going to pan out that way. Frank didn't like pity though, and I bet his legs are working great again, wherever he may be.

Albert and I return to Los Angeles after the holiday and begin pulling ourselves back together. We have funerals to attend to and a brand new year to begin. Raul comes by so we can catch-up on our holiday trips, and I tell him the same thing I'm telling you.

Raul had worked at Fountain View on Christmas Day. I now realize that the name of the institution comes from the street name "Fountain" that it's located on, and not a water-feature, so the view is of traffic. Pretty. I ask him how his day went.

"It was mostly volunteers working with me. Do you know who volunteers on Christmas day?" he asks.

"I would imagine mostly really nice non-Christians." I respond.

"Yes, mostly young Jewish girls. They had a blast handing out the presents to all the residents, and wearing the red fur hats. It was crazy," he says laughing.

It was a holiday I will never forget. Fanny and Frank both passed away. Dad had a battle with his own body and won. I learned the real origins of my family's business, and for a group of seniors in Hollywood, Santa Claus was a little Jewish girl.

The End

ABOUT THE AUTHOR

Billy Lambrinides is a writer and art director living in Hollywood, California. He is currently working on a collection of true short stories. He publishes a blog online at www.OutLikeaLamb.com

CPSIA information can be obtained at www.ICGtesting.com
Printed in the USA
BVOW03s1133250813

329492BV00011B/338/P